Seeking

MO

by

Scott Gibson

With grateful thanks to my friend and pen pal James T. Spartz for his support and contributions to this endeavor, to my father and stepmother Ray and Kathy Gibson for their constant encouragement, and to my son Thomas Gibson for his patience during the completion of this book.

This book is based on a series of actual letters written between friends when they were in their twenties. Some names, places, and employers have been changed to protect privacy.

On the day of this typing, this day in history, February 8, 2014, the United States Attorney General Eric Holder announced sweeping changes in the Justice Department's handling of same sex married couples, including granting all of the same legal federal rights as opposite sex couples.

Edited by Scott Gibson
Blood & Tears, Poems for Matthew Shepard
Painted Leaf Press, NYC 1999

Also by Scott Gibson
Sticked Stoned & Bottled
New Shrine, Boulder CO 2014

SCOTT GIBSON

Seeking

MO

A Spiritual Journey

Mystic Steeple
Boulder Colorado

Mystic Steeple
A division of Omnia Om Ltd.

For permissions, contact the Publisher:
omniaom.com/contact

Cover design by Scott Gibson. Cover photo by Matt Bridger/DHD Multimedia Gallery: http://gallery.hd.org

ISBN: 978-1-942378-01-3

for Abe

SEEKING MO

58.
Dear Mom,

This is my suicide note to you.

I'm not sorry for it by the way, and I'll explain all that to you here. I'll explain why I'm not going to worry about how you feel anymore, why I don't care if you miss me or not, or if I was ever right in your eyes.

I understand that parents want to be proud of their kids, and growing up, I used to try, desperately, to live my life so that both you and dad would be proud of me. I learned there are specific ways to act, things to say, and ambitions that were rewarded more than others, and I tried to change to align myself with those ideals in order to enhance my popularity, to be accepted in small-town Slinger and in your home.

But it never felt right. I was athletic only because you and dad expected that of me. Did you know I also wanted to be an actor? No, I didn't think you knew that.

After years of wondering, of knowing deep down but trying to figure out what it was and why (why, why) I felt this way, I finally came to terms with being gay. What a huge mountain to climb! But I only wanted to feel good, to feel normal.

I SO desperately wanted to talk to you, Mom, but every time I tried you just made me feel worse. When I was finally able to lift my head again, inevitably you'd cut me down and make me feel like I was worthless again. It has been a cycle that I don't care to repeat ever again.

You used to tell me that I needed to stop being selfish, to stop wanting to fornicate with other men, and get right with God. Even when I said I couldn't help my feelings and that God made me like this, you told me that God gave me this challenge, this temptation in life that I needed to overcome. Even when I told you that I just wanted to fall in love, that I can't fall IN love with a woman, you told me that God wanted me to suffer in this life, in order to learn a lesson.

All this BS that you fed me forced me to seek God even more, to study the Bible, to study the history of the Christian church, religion in general, to study other religions, to figure out who I really am. I asked you several times to join me, to study the Aramaic language, to seek the original source in order to find Christ's true message. I asked you to read literature about homosexuality, other than that published by the church, to examine scientific studies, to seek further information in order to be more educated about this major issue that your very own flesh and blood was having to come to grips with. But you never did—you only sought the counsel of your church leaders.

Interestingly, I loved you so much that I was the only one out of all your kids who would come and visit you, who would spend time with you when I was in town—who gave you the time of day, really. Yet, you just kept judging me, trying to set me "straight" (to set me back), to tell me I was selfish for seeking the love of my life.

I have come to understand that my own lack of selfishness, trying to be who <u>you</u> wanted me to be, trying to accomplish what <u>you</u> hoped for me, was only feeding <u>your</u> selfishness. You wanted me to conform to <u>your</u> visions of my life. You wanted me to please <u>you</u>.

I have finally learned that trying to please you denies me <u>my</u> life, it denies who <u>I</u> really am. And what a waste of my life that has been!

I've got great news for you, Mom. This is my suicide note to you because I love you. This is my suicide note to you because I want you to learn, because this is what's best for you, for us both. This is my suicide note to you because I am being selfish, finally.

You don't have to live my life anymore. You can live your own life and not have to worry about me. That's how much I love you.

Goodbye.
Marc

Wait. I need to go back. This journey begins long before Marc's goodbye, long before his final letter to his mother.

I will begin late in his college career. As I write, I am using a stack of letters written by JT and Marc, which they began to exchange on September 5, 1995, immediately after their trip. I have supplemented the letters with information I learned about Marc through conversations I've had with Jack.

To give a bit of context, the Internet was in its infancy. Marc had recently paid $800 for a used DOS computer with a CRT monitor, after debating at length the merits of a computer that ran DOS versus one with Windows.

The final semester or two of his undergrad degree, Marc had been required by the university to dabble with email, which actually led to more frustration among most of the students than anything else. They already had enough to read with textbooks and copied handouts, and now email added thirty-five student responses to every one of the professor's prompts, plus any rebuttals some of the idiots felt they needed to include.

But there was no digital communication between Marc and Jack. No cell phones, no email, no texts. They exchanged letters for about fifteen months during which time they sought refuge in their memories of camaraderie. I am a friend and pen pal who came later, after Marc and Jack's history concluded. But we'll get to that.

Using these letters as a guide, I attempt to portray the development of a genuine friendship. It is a casual yet sincere display of truth and trust as they manage the complexities of friendships and lovers, family, and meaningful jobs (or lack thereof), while constantly

12

questioning the nature of God, humanity, and societal institutions in the hope of finding their lives' true paths.

I try to stay true to the format, the feeling, and the content of the letters; however, I gloss over some of the more cringe-worthy lines such as "we'd let her be, then on the road again with glee." I'm sure there are other lines readers may feel I should have ditched as well, but I leave many in to highlight Jack and Marc's human qualities as they grow and mature on their journeys of self discovery. I have changed the names of some of the people, places and employers in the letters in order to protect their privacy.

One more note regarding Marc and JT's story. They drank a lot of beer, perhaps Marc more than Jack, but Jack supplemented his drinking with a good deal of high quality grass. He seems to have had a tough time calling it by name, but there it was, in the background, most of the time.

A week before school started, they fiddled with JT's new guitar and old conga drum inside his dusty, two bedroom apartment four blocks from campus. Jack smoked American Spirit, a step up from Marc's former brand, Camel Lights, which he had smoked only ten days earlier. Quitting took all the effort he had, and he'd hoped he could stick with it.

Jack had graduated from the University of Wisconsin - La Crosse in May, and Marc was awaiting his final semester as an undergrad to commence in September. He was a bit behind since he'd had too much fun his Freshman year and took a short hiatus to experience life before returning to school.

"I wish I knew someone who could ride with me, share some of the driving, you know," Jack stated outright, a bit out of the blue. Marc sensed a bit of fear creeping into his friend.

They had met in an Understanding Human Differences class at UW-L, a class where each student's prejudices were exposed each week within discussions that would usually provoke barroom brawls. Jack was a smallish, long-haired blond who sat in the back of the class, his eyes focused on the back of the young man in front of him as if reading the back of his t-shirt. This meditative state gave the illusion of disinterest until once each class Jack would serve his opinion, like adding pepperoni to a peanut butter and jelly.

Jack was moving to southern Arizona, far away from what he called "the total bullshit" of a relationship just ended. It was a long drive, especially for a small-town Midwestern boy just out of college.

Somehow the statement made Marc's head jerk, an imperceptible twitch. It was meant to be, the one moment it was all defined, when fate just grabbed him, controlled his voice, and set the whole thing into motion. "I'll drive with you," he said.

Of course as a college student, Marc's bank account didn't show more than $20, so he had to ask his roommate Jen to borrow some cash until his student loan landed. Marc had known Jen for a few years, and they'd shared an apartment since Marc had birthed into his gay life about a year prior. Jen trusted him, considered him the most moral of any of her friends, so the decision to lend him a couple hundred bucks was an easy one.

Once in hand, a quick visit to the travel agent secured Marc a one-way ticket from Phoenix back to La Crosse. It didn't take long for his whole life to change.

The Caprice was packed so full that Marc had to sit cross-legged in the passenger seat during the first leg. Sleeping was near impossible. They headed out about 10PM

14

on a late August night, two buddies seeking new experiences.

Jack's 1985 Chevy Caprice Classic drove on balding tires and pulled a bit to the right. "It shimmies a bit around 55," Jack liked to say, "but it straightens out again around 80." It was a dry sense of humor.

The air conditioner definitely did not work.

Too wired to sleep, Marc joined Jack singing the hit songs of the times, Hootie and the Blowfish, Tom Petty, Indigo Girls, Neil Young unplugged, as the half moon rose above. West Interstate 90 lifted them across the Mississippi then climbed over the western bluffs and into Minnesota. I90 met I35 South, and halfway through Iowa they merged onto Interstate 80 which brought them west across the Missouri River at Omaha and into Nebraska. The waxing moon and starlight added to the enchantment of the night.

Marc dozed for an hour or two, but his driving shift came way too early. *Good thing country music is easy to stay awake to,* he thought, and good thing JT was one of those music loving, anything works for me, kind of guys. The country music, Garth Brooks, Reba, Brooks and Dunn and the Boot Scootin' Boogie, worked for a while, but eventually a tired driver needs some other sort of stimulation: Beastie Boys, Public Enemy, *Rust Never Sleeps*.

At the next fill-up, the cashier rang up a large coffee and a hard pack of Camel Lights. After almost two weeks of not smoking, Marc admitted the cigarettes tasted pretty good, especially on the road with a hot cup of black coffee and his good buddy falling asleep in the passenger seat beside him.

There was no itinerary, no agenda. They had driven the night and planned to drive most of the next day, see where they ended up, find a campsite, and if time permitted, explore any interesting towns nearby. On their journey, they

15

would see Boulder, Pueblo, Santa Fe, Gallup, and Payson. The best of the best was two nights at Christopher Creek Campground in Arizona's Tonto National Forest. Crisp summer evening air was new for these Midwesterners. They breathed it in upon the pine-breath blanket of the Arizona mountains. It was a nice surprise finding Chris's Creek, but we'll get to that in a bit.

Like their role models before them, they were on the road. On their first night after leaving La Crosse, Marc and Jack camped in the foothills west of Pueblo, Colorado. The crickets chirped loudly, and the giant trees pissed their energy upon them (that's a line from JT's recap of their adventure). They absorbed every bit of that energy like all else in the natural world.

In the morning, they arose, did their duties in the woods, brushed their teeth with warm beer, and had a quick dip in the cold creek. In no time, they wound their way back down the mountain, heavy on the brake pedal, and headed south again.

Even though the night air is much colder in the southwest, the summer day and the retreat from the foothills inspired significant heat driving south on I25 into New Mexico. Without air conditioning, the windows were open wide. The dry heat leached the sweat and the remaining alcohol from their bodies.

Around midday, they cruised Trinidad, the Mexican shops and museums, the cafes. They dined at La Fiesta. Jack had french fries with mayo at the Mexican café, washed down with coffee and a cigarette.

He released the burdens of La Crosse. In the woods the night before, Jack had, for the first time, spoken to Marc specifically about his break up and his motivations for moving to the desert. He explained that he felt the need to leave La Crosse in order to "cleanse his mind and soul after

16

spending so many months dodging a stalking ex-friend." But now he was on to new things.

Santa Fe welcomed them with an open spirit. The Advocate magazine sold proudly at the Galisteo News, where they dined for coffee and lunch alongside an elderly couple reading the Pasatiempo. Something just felt good there, in Santa Fe. After lunch, they strolled through the plaza, visiting the New Mexico Museum of Art, the Cathedral of St. Francis of Assisi, the Palace of the Governors, a couple Native American art galleries, and the Georgia O'Keefe Museum. Mid afternoon, with reluctance, they pulled out of town heading west.

Their next stop was for a pee at a rustic, lazy saloon and gas station along Interstate 40. Two old men with sunken eyes and leathery skin visited on a bench out front. Somehow Marc had a feeling he should check the tires on the old Chevy, and fortunately he did. A large bubble was forming from beneath the worn tread on the front driver's side tire. They discussed it at length and felt the urgency to change her out.

The Caprice had an even older spare packed underneath everything in "a trunk big enough to hold four bodies" as Jack liked to say. Though the rubber on the spare tire was old and cracking in most places, it held air and was full sized, so they went ahead and jacked up the Chevy in the full heat of the southwestern sun, changed the tire, then repacked the stereo speakers, clothes, and box upon box of miscellaneous books and music cd's. In 45 minutes, they were again making tracks to the Arizona border.

Rather than heading to Flagstaff and then up to the Grand Canyon and finally back down to Phoenix, a more direct route would prove safer, they thought. So south out of Holbrook down State Highway 377 they went.

17

What a hidden gem! What a secret! Who knew Arizona was so beautiful!

At first they shared pleasant jabs, when they saw the signs announcing the Apache-Sitgreaves National Forest, teasing about what a "National Forest" looks like in Arizona as they drove past the barrel cactus and sagebrush.

Soon, signs littered the road asking, "Do you want to kill your wife and kids?" and warning of "Elk on Road." What was all of this poetic roadside preaching? Why in this odd little group of bushes in the middle of Nowhere, Arizona were there signs that read, "Your speed, you choose. Hit an elk, you both lose"?

Then, out of nowhere, the road dropped off the Mogollon Rim, and down they went into the clouds. Finally they appeared, enormous, gracious, a community of wild beasts. The elk grazed along the road and in the forest beside. A bull and two cows strolled straight up the lane. Marc fumbled for the camera as Jack drove at a slowish pace.

Soon the road flattened and then rose up again into the Arizona mountains, twisting and turning through the pines. They found Christopher Creek Campground in Tonto National Forest just northeast of Payson. They knew why it was a national forest now—and not one joke about looking for the Lone Ranger during their entire two-night stay.

They settled in to their site, in awe of their surroundings. Having grown up in Wisconsin, Marc had only ever known Arizona as a hot desert that grandparents retired to and his neighbors visited to develop tans during spring break. The soul-searching and mind-enlightening conversation he shared with Jack, along with all the beer they drank, only enhanced the joy Marc felt in Arizona's nature.

Marc found his peace in searching for God, although he had recently developed a difficult time talking about

God, and "peace" was a relative term. He felt embarrassed now, not that he minded talking about God, but he worried that people would think he was a closed-minded, judgmental, and angry zealot. He had always been taught to fear God, to be concerned about His wrath, and to prepare for judgment day.

Jack found his passion in music, lyrics, and song. He admitted to creating songs at the of age of eight in order to keep himself entertained during his walks to and from school in the small Minnesota town where he was raised. He hadn't yet begun to get serious about his passion for songwriting when they sat by the fire at Christopher Creek, but it brewed inside of him.

I am writing this book in homage, two decades removed from the formative adventures of these men. I have never met Marc—I only know him through his letters to Jack, my friend who was kind enough to share their exchanges with me for this endeavor.

I have to admit that I have learned a great deal about myself through my examination of Marc's life and his relationship with our mutual friend. Everything Marc had been taught told me, as I read through his letters, that he was raised in a very similar environment to me, with many shared experiences: small town values, middle-class parents, religious mother, etc. Jack tells me that Marc and I are spiritual doppelgangers, except for the slight accent Marc had developed from his Chilean-born father. For this reason, to explore vicariously my own personal history and growth, I have been inspired to write this book.

That we are here on this earth to perfect ourselves in order to be prepared for Heaven had been taught to both Marc and me, all our lives, not only by our mothers, but by our friends, our friends' parents, our teachers and our coaches. As I read through his letters, I see Marc struggling almost daily with the concepts of Heaven and God and Sin. *But we are all sinners*, Marc often thought, and he asked these questions to his elders too, always with the response that if you go to God and ask Him for forgiveness, then all your sins are forgiven and your ticket into Heaven will be secured.

Marc often told himself and others, in a joking way of course, that on his deathbed, he would definitely ask God for forgiveness and then hope he died immediately after that for fear that the lovely nurse would waltz in and he'd suddenly have an unclean thought just before he died. If that happened, he'd go straight to Hell, of course.

I just might not win this one no matter how hard I try, he thought. *Is it fate that the nurse walks in at the last moment? Was I created by God just to go to Hell? If that's the case, what's the use in living in the first place?* Like me, Marc was constantly trying to figure stuff out, doing the soul-work to make life make sense. He needed to know the inner workings of things, the meanings and justifications, and why they were the way they were.

When he was in middle school, he began to meditate in bed. He didn't call it meditation; it was relaxation, self hypnosis, guided first by pleasant voices on an audio tape until he got good at it and could practice by himself. He'd begin at his toes, focus on them and feel them relax, the tension melt away. Then he'd slowly move up his body, placing his awareness in each muscle and feeling them relax before moving up to the next muscle. Though he wasn't sure why, he always felt better, more focused, calm, and able to maintain his attention on his school work after he meditated.

Regarding God, Christianity taught both Marc and me that a major component of being Christian is having Faith! Faith that God will answer prayers is understandable, but having been taught to dread judgment day, Faith that God will not strike us down with determined vengeance because we may have had an unclean thought about the young nurse who was probably married (which also adds adultery in His book) was hard to chew. God-forbid the nurse would be male—talk about difficult to swallow! He was dead already; it was useless. Marc certainly had Faith in that.

Jack and Marc had these conversations. In La Crosse, Marc had attended Campus Crusade for Christ meetings, Bible studies, and group prayers. Jack was a psych major, a well-read and thoughtful one, if not a little too self-conscious, which seemed to make it okay for Marc to discuss these questions about God with him. He'd tried to ask some of these same probing questions to his friends in CCC and his Bible study groups, and the only "conversation" he'd ever gotten was actually the one conversation stopper they would always pull out: "You just have to have Faith."

But Jack joined Marc in trying to figure things out, to talk things through, questioning the authority of the "great thinkers" of the past. "They were human too," he'd say, "which means they had issues just like the rest of us. You can't judge them for that." Marc loved this about Jack, the fact that he was so open, the fact that he didn't judge Marc for being gay, that he constantly questioned his own beliefs as well as others, trying to improve himself each day of his life.

The first morning at Christopher Creek, they arose with some aching heads that cleared up pretty quickly in the fresh, mountain air. They spoke to the campsite attendant, asked her if there was anything nearby they definitely had to see. She told them about Box Canyon, about an hour's walk down the creek; they packed up some sandwiches, water, and cigarettes and began their adventure.

Eventually, the stream widened slightly and began dropping into pools. Waterfall after waterfall cascaded into pool after pool. Other people had already made their way there; Marc and Jack assumed there must have been other routes to Box Canyon. Following the lead of others, it didn't take long for the two to launch themselves off a stone wall. They spent the afternoon jumping from rock walls into cool pools of mountain water. The excitement even topped the elk they had seen the day before.

That night, relaxed, rejuvenated, they enjoyed some beers and smokes and sang the entire album of Neil Diamond's *Hot August Night*. As the moon rose and they lied back on their bags, heads propped up on logs, a sort of melancholy set in.

They were restless in the morning, packing up their gear, stuffing the car full yet again, the beetles the size of coffee mugs.

At the airport in Phoenix, they shook hands, then with only a brief hesitation, hugged their goodbyes. Though quick, the trip had been a pilgrimage of exploration, revelation, and transition. Inside Sky Harbor International, they wondered aloud if they would meet again. They decided they would at least write, but Marc questioned inside whether he would fulfill his promise. He had made this agreement in the past, with a German exchange student in high school, with his grandmother, with a friend he had met on vacation at Birch Lake, agreements that were never followed through.

A good man, thought Marc. At least he'd had the chance to know him.

It didn't take long for JT to write. A week into Marc's final semester at UW-L, he received the first of many letters from his wandering friend. Their letters are now their memories, many forgotten until dusting these old things off. They are letters of their desperation to find meaning in life, of their challenges finding love and direction throughout their years, of relationships that were and those that were almost.

From the very first letter, there is contemplation of spirit, of life, of finding out who they are or who they are trying to be. Through their choices of music, books, employment, education, and family, their worlds would slowly open up and quickly close.

1.
Marcus:

Hello my On The Road man! How is everything going? Very well (still) I hope. Things are going well down here. I applied for a couple of jobs and a few more tomorrow. Mostly employment working with emotionally disturbed kids and/or delinquent youth.

It has been a little "lonely," but all I have to do is think about what I don't have to deal with on a day-to-day basis down here as compared to La Crosse. Makes me feel a lot better. I feel good. I bought the *Basic Writings of C.G. Jung* today. Very intriguing, from a student of psychology & spirituality point of view. I also bought and read *The Alchemist* by Paulo Coehlo; nice little fable. Jung has written some on Alchemy and its relation to psychology and spirituality. I haven't read it but saw it in the bookstore.

How is the play coming? Excellent I hope. I want to see a video or at least mail me a script so I can read it, finally! Take care. I will write more later. Write if you feel the urge.

Miss Ya,
Peace,
Jack

2.
Marc:

Hey, what's up? Just a quick note here to explain something.

It occurred to me recently that you're of the spirit of: emotion = do, while I am of the: think, think, plan, plan, and maybe someday shit will happen. I dig your spirit, but somehow I have a rough time with such things. I hope to learn from you.

Anyhow, I remember our conversation about God while we were camping on our trip, the night in Colorado, and I've been thinking quite a bit about it recently. We had been discussing the universe and how it seems to keep going and going, never-ending. You had said something about getting to the end of it (the universe) and then like sticking your head out through God's skin (or something) and seeing what's beyond the darkness. Then I said something like, "why don't you just kill yourself right now, get it over with, and find out all the answers of the universe."

Well, please don't do that. You know I was just kidding. I'd hoped you'd see the irony of the fact that all of us will die in the future, soon enough you know, and if you make it happen too quickly, you'd miss out on all the cool parts like experiencing life and trying to figure stuff out. The search for self and the soul have been common themes since the beginning of humanity. It's sort of cool thinking about it. It makes me feel like all the "required" bullshit is a waste of time. You know, getting the education, having a fam, living vicariously through your kids, following all the normal stuff parents and society engrain in you from the start. Seems like a waste when the whole world is out there. I'm thinking we should see more, experience more, and if it takes buying an off-road vehicle to get there, then so be it. I want one. Call me greedy!

Sounds like fun, don't you think? Besides, if you killed yourself, I'd miss ya.

So don't.

That's all.
Write.
Jack

3.
My man Ortega, what is going on?

Did you get my first couple of mailings? I hope so. Pictures turned out okay, especially the one sunset and that one of you with the sun on your back outside of Santa Fe. Anyway, I wrote this stuff and want your feedback. I'm not sure why I want feedback, probably because I don't have anyone around here and because I trust and value your judgment.

I got a job, pending a physical exam and drug screen tomorrow. Both should be fine (trust me). It is at a house for youth (boys) that are in between juvi hall and a stable home. I get some benefits and not so much pay, but it will be a good experience.

I picked up Dostoevsky's *Crime and Punishment* the other day. Finished it. Yeah right. This should take me a while. Good thing I'm also reading about 5 other books! Picked up some of the most excellent music today. Professor Longhair. He is THE New Orleans piano man. He inspired a whole school of musicians including Dr. John. Very piano-rockin'-boogie-woogie-jazzy-blues. The shit. Instant classic & most cherished edition to my collection.

Value what you have, love and surroundings.
–Ferron

Meditation (mindfulness) paves the road to discovery of the self. Awareness of the uniqueness of one and one's own journey bestows the courage to follow and discover the endless possibilities of life. –Me

These are two affirmations on my dry erase right now.

Livin' & Learnin.'

Take care.
Peace and Good Music.
Jack

P.S. Here's that writing:

Success is what I fear
        It is also what I aim for
Unconscious and indeterminable as to cause
        But effect is
Noncompletion, labeled as
        Underachievement
Do the right thing
        Gain feelings worthy of praise
Frightening and unfamiliar
Internal confrontation has held me back
        And held me up
From diving in and
        Getting wet all over
        Soaking myself in attainment
But now, raised into consciousness, my will
        Will build me up on my self alone
Responsible and cognizant
Of where I am going
        Although
I do not know my destination
        I am a mountain unto myself
The crest of that hill, I will
        Reach out and know

The psychic nature of instinct
        Clashing and combating
Willful freedom of choice
Conscious responsibility taken for

27

>>Actions meticulously or impulsively
>Captured in stride
>>On the way to self discovery
>Will
>>Will make the difference
>Forces of nature
>>Assist me in my journey
>Carry my spirit as I
>>Help myself to my destiny

4.
Hi Jack!

Just what I've been pondering lately: They say our spirits leave our bodies for a few minutes each night to go explore this and other worlds without the restriction of our physical bodies. Then they say that the reason we have difficulties willing our souls to leave our bodies while we are conscious is because we and our bodies are afraid (unconsciously) that our souls will not return—thus, we are dead—I thought I was through with my fear of death, but, obviously, it must be an instinctual, ever-present fear of what is consciously unknown.

What is interesting, Jack, is that last night I began thinking and writing (a little) about this. Upon waking this morning, I realized I've been having a recurring dream about fear—I believe it was about all fear, but it was being expressed in the dream as my fear of heights. The dream setting: some sort of water park. The problem: must climb minimally protected open stairs (ladders) to get to the start of the slide.

Previously I had gotten stuck on the more difficult route to the top (there are two routes). I usually had no problem on the second route until last night. There is one unprotected ladder at the top—with only 3 rungs—which until this point, I'd only slightly hesitated on. Last night I got stuck—I couldn't move—people were climbing over me—around me—I'm surprised they didn't go through me. So, JT boy, what do you suppose all of this means?

I got your pictures—very cool stuff—thanks. Just yesterday I directed a monologue from my play *Janet,* about a woman desperately seeking her life's love. Awesome energy comes from seeing your own creation come to life. I think I know how new fathers feel!

So all the energy I soaked up while we were on the road has been drained. I've been a bitch lately. For example, I've noticed myself walking by people and instead of saying, "Hi," I'd think, *What the hell are you looking at?* Now what kind of an attitude is that? Filled with energy means filled with love. I guess I don't have a lot of energy left—I try like hell to find 15 minutes between classes or some other time to meditate, but it seems I've always got other things to do. Your letters help a lot though.

Just listen to me complain. I even went to the bank and bought checks with nature scenes on them so whenever I write one out, I can relax and enjoy the view.

I have a poetry reading at Red Oak Books on Friday night. I'm trying to come up with a theme for it. We'll see how it goes.

That picture of me glowing is kind of interesting cuz I'd just gotten done meditating and soaking up the Nat'l forest's energy.

Keep writing. Miss you.
Marc.

P.S. Art thou a non puffer/exhalator? Almost 3 weeks for me. Yeehah country bumpkin.

Jack was a psychology major in college, which both enhanced their interesting conversations and also set Marc up for what was to come in his next letter. He should have known not to ask Jack to analyze his dream. He knew Jack had just picked up that Jung book.

5.
Hello Marcky!

You know, I am not much (at all) for dream interpretation. Let me consult C.G. Jung...

"Stereotyped interpretation of dream-motifs is to be avoided; the only justifiable interpretations are those reached through a painstaking examination of the context. Even if one has great experience in these matters, one is again and again obliged, before each dream, to admit one's ignorance and, renouncing all preconceived ideas, to prepare for something entirely unexpected...

"...the concept of <u>compensation</u> seemed to me the only adequate one, for it alone is capable of summing up all the various ways in which a dream behaves...

"...I must therefore refer the reader to my book *Psychology and Alchemy*, which contains an investigation into the structure of a dream-series with special reference to the individuation process."

Well, Jung had some very interesting things to say. What I just wrote was from *Collected Works, Volume 8: The Structure and Dynamics of the Psyche.* (Princeton University Press, 1970.) Generally, I have no idea what your dream (or series of) would represent. I would suggest checking out (in what little spare time you have) the Psych. and Alchemy book. Jung is a pretty DEEP cat. Not to be ingested in large quantities in short periods of time.

I would, generally, (maybe!?!) address it—your dream—as an anxiety (neurosis) (irrational fear) associated with heights, physical or metaphysical (or of success—the play?—achieving a desired goal?). But I wouldn't feel comfortable in any analyst position. Not with such little experience.

Let's see what else you've been pondering. The fear of death. Not an altogether uncommon fear. Self-preservation is a healthy and worthwhile attribute. Just a thought... wouldn't the consciously unknown (as you said) also be the unconsciously known? Just a little thought I had while reading your letter. A fear diminishing after conscious projection of spirit out of our bodies? A very interesting concept. One that may take some time to mull over in my melon. Thanks for the fuel.

I am so glad to hear your play is coming together so well. God damn I wish I were there to see it. At least send me a script so I can read it. The development of an original creation through full fruition. What a joy that must be! I am very proud of you, my man. Continued good luck!

About your energy, it occurred to me that it doesn't seem that you're so much <u>low</u> on energy as you may be filled with an energy that is much more negative (-) than positive (+). It can be difficult to turn. I know that! I can see why it's there though. Anxiety (unconscious) about the play, senioritis, and a heavy class load will not only wear a person's energy down, but it will build up that negative energy too.

What I try to do is think of the positives when I can. Like consider your life, really: You have your health (1) the birth of a brain child (your play) (2) almost a degree (3) smart (4) articulate (5) handsome (6) and on and on. You got it going on—give yourself some deserved credit.

Keep trying to find that time to yourself. You <u>MUST READ</u> this book (I am in the process). It is the <u>PERFECT</u> book for you right now. *Wherever You Go, There You Are: Mindfulness Meditation in Everyday Life* by Jon Kabat-Zinn. A MUST READ. If you have read it already, read it again.

Good luck on your poetry reading. I bought *Pomes All Sizes* the other day in a used bookstore. It is a posthumously published book of Kerouac poetry, forward by Allen Ginsberg. I like it.

Keep your chin up man; what goes around comes around (Yin/Yang).

I start training at my new job tomorrow. It should be interesting to say the least. I bought a six-string Fender acoustic. Love it.

Take it easier!
Jack

6.
Hi Jackson,

I have climbed slowly into the school groove and am finally, I believe, enjoying learning again. I wish, however, I could study what I want to—on my own, you know—granted a lot of what we're reading does ROCK—Emerson, Thoreau, Whitman— transcendentalist stuff, which coincides with my new era of thought these days.

You were right about the positive (+) and negative (-) energy thing. I believe the negative energy was created by an overload in my schedule. 15 credits in 3 days is a lot to handle, especially when you procrastinate as much as I do. My Monday, Tuesday, and Wednesday nights were full of nothing but studying late. However, I have taken action steps to solve my problem of negative (lack of) energy. I dumped my directing class, and the play won't be produced. I really wanted to do it, but I'm just too busy. Or, perhaps you're right. Maybe unconsciously I really didn't want to do it. Maybe I don't feel worthy of seeing it through to fruition.

I had mentioned it in a phone conversation with my mom a couple weeks back. She told me to make sure I told her when it was being presented so she could try to get up here to see it. Maybe that's why I (unconsciously) sabotaged it. By the way, she also told me that it was not up to her to tell me whether or not I am going to Hell because that's between me and God. She says she loves me more than anyone else except Jesus. Not sure about that one. What I AM sure of though is that I'm too busy right now to produce a play.

I'm considering moving out of my current apartment situation in order to enjoy some solo living for the last few months of my undergraduate career (which might help me focus more on my studies and therefore free up some much needed time). It will be difficult to tell Jen, but her boy Ben's really a bummer right now, lying around the house (which is not even his) like a blob. I like listening to John Denver when he's there. It tends to drive him nuts.

Hey, I've also discovered an interesting little book which needs much thought with every page (every line perhaps). It's called *Prayers of the Cosmos: Meditations on the Aramaic Words of Jesus* by Neil Douglas Klotz (Harper San Francisco 1990).

Evidently, the Aramaic language is quite ambiguous, and the translations in the Bible are only the accepted translations of one person or group of people many, many, many years ago, probably translated to accommodate the beliefs and agendas of the translators of that time (or whoever they were translating for). For example, "God" in Aramaic also means "the One" and "Heaven" is a state of mind—being filled with love and joy—it is NOT a specific place.

Maybe when we die and go into the light, which is just a vibrant vibration of love and joy. You know like when your heart sings with love and joy. We've GOT to be all consciousness, you know? According to this book, Jesus never used words with gender, and it was all about light, sound, vibration, and energy. Amazing knowledge within that skull. Pretty sure he studied Eastern philosophy, religion, and meditation. Pretty sure Jesus was a mystic. Chew on that a while. I think my mom would LOVE this book…NOT.

I've decided I'm going to take a semester off (at least) after graduation to look at schools, travel, whatever, before hitting grad school for Creative Writing. A teacher told me to consider the University of Arizona, as they apparently have a good poetry program there. Perhaps I could come visit and take a look.

Your new job sounds cool. That could be part of your forte, you know. Working with kids I mean—practicing patience.

Talk to you later.

This is Jesus speaking here:

"Tubwayhun layleyn d'kaphneen watzheyn l'khenuta d'hinnon nisbhun."

–"Aligned with the One are those who wait up at night, weakened and dried out inside by the <u>unnatural</u> state of the world; they shall receive satisfaction" (Klotz 56).

"Tubwayhun layleyn dadkeyn blebhon d'hinnon nehzun l'alaha."

KJV: "Blessed are the pure in heart: for they shall see God."

Other possibility: "Healthy are those whose passion is electrified by deep, abiding purpose [love and friendship]; they shall regard the power that moves and shows itself in all things" (Klotz 62).

Take care.
Marc

7.
Marcky,

So there I was, knee deep in rice cakes and deafened by Meatloaf muzac with a hairdresser in a short hot-pink skirt and heels on one side and three vertically challenged circus clowns on the other. We rode the Greyhound express through America's Heartland

36

and eventually found ourselves flowing over Niagra Falls in separate wood barrels, except for me (I had to share mine with two of the three clowns). Damn, that was a trip!

How are you? John Denver is cool. My mom was a fan. I had a double LP (live) of his, but as with all my LP's, it was ruined when I left them sit on the floor of my cabin.

So, you would recommend Whitman-Emerson-Thoreau? What exactly is a transcendentalist? I picked up some new reading for myself. Some Bukowski, Anias Nin, LeRoi Jones, H. Rap Brown (the last two big in the Black Power movement in the 70's). I also picked up some poetry: Nikki Giovanni, Carl Sandburg.

I received your pictures. I liked them, esp. the Box Canyon ones. Have you found a new pad yet? Living alone has its advantages. My favorite happens to be the unrestricted option of strutting around nude whenever I damn well please.

I love my guitar. I play it all the time even at work (which is now an overnight shift which allows me plenty of picking—strumming—plucking—reading and even a little cable viewing and movie watching time).

Perfection is illusion. Too much moderation is in itself an extreme.

Sip tea.
Watch mountains shine
in morning light.

Differences compliment individuality, accentuate
wholeness.

Be good—be well.
Jack

8.
Dear JT,

Sounds like you had a hell of a trip down the falls.
I've got a few hours before class, and I'm trying to
revise some poems since I don't have enough to read
on Friday night.

Say, there's an attractive guy that just started
working with me at the Lux Queen, and I need a
little advice. What would you do if a guy asked you
out? Would you get pissed? Of course you're lax
about that. Somebody else might be totally opposite.
We've been "looking into each other's eyes" I think,
so maybe it's possible.

Not sure if I've told you, but the UW-L gay support
group puts together an Oktoberfest weekend get-
together/dance each year, which is cool. It was last
night—my friend Dave and I went for a little while,
and it was fine, a good idea really for the 18-20
crowd. Not so much for us legals, you know, since
we've got Memories, the local gay bar, to go to.

But as we were leaving, there was this guy who had just realized he was at the wrong party, and he just started <u>freaking out</u> and screaming, "Fucking Faggots. You Fucking Gay Fucking Homos..." non stop and at the top of his lungs like they were taking his youngest child away from him. Well, Dave and I got the heck out of there (SCARY—VOLATILE) and went down to the real Oktoberfest and had fun.

I got up early this morning and am a bit shaky. Not sure how I got home, but I think maybe I was home pretty early since I got up so early. I hope I didn't do anything too stupid.

I found my new apartment. It's above Estaban's downtown (and a short walk from the Oktoberfestivities). It's a big one bedroom with a new fridge and a garbage disposal. The building also has a sauna and a raquetball court. I'm extremely excited about the move. I think maybe that's what my dream was about since once I told Jen I was moving out, I made it to the top of that slide in my recurring dream. I think maybe I felt like I was being held back from learning by still living in this apartment. I love Jen and all, but her slug of a boyfriend is here even when she's not. Gotta be tired of that. Maybe I'm wrong though (about the dream).

No words of inspiration this time, although my mom says she still loves me even though I'm gay (so that's good eh?). But she also says (in the same breath pretty much) that I'm probably going to Hell, since only those who have given their lives over to

Jesus are filled with the Holy Spirit and are going to get into Heaven.

Those poor spiritless Buddhists! They just don't know what's coming. Oh, and don't forget all the African kids dying of starvation. Those poor kids dealt with Hell on Earth and then, POW, right to Hell after they die cuz they never got to know Jesus. That sucks.

Keep writing soon.
Marc.

9.
Mack,

So, there I was, caught between thoughts of objective disassociation from value judgments being placed on other people, or groups, in contrast to personal opinion (and how both are justified); and the entire Modeling/Fashion industry as a major contributor to the decline of Western Civilization, when it hit me: I could give up this quest for truth, integrity, and wisdom and regress into a mind-numbingly dull existence of Joe Redneck which has, as its only forms of cognitive challenge, the debate between regular or light beer, what time to watch Jerry Springer, and whether or not to put a new gun rack in the truck.

But then I realized THAT lifestyle is definitely not for me, personally.

"I am building a mountain unto myself," I thought, the peak only reached after a lifetime of deep intellectual searching countered with striving for life in the Moment, a life of Flow. Then I realized I'm not building a mountain within myself. Mountains are not built; they are discovered (well, they are formed geologically by physical force, plate tectonics, etc.— and that of course can be analogized to the sexual unification of male and female to form child—but that's a different story).

What we are dealing with here is the discovery of the preexisting space of self-awareness and sense of true identity that many (most) people spend at least some time exploring. Some climb, some stop. Some make it all the way to the top (Buddha? Christ??).

But I, as a traveler, a vagabond wanderer, in the cognitive sense, continue to climb the mountain range within. I discover its vast extent, its challenges, its beauty. I attempt to harness its power and progress from it. Absorb, deny, climb, wonder. I expand as I discover each mountain meadow and spring-fed lake. I continue to learn, to climb. I find ego and reject it and then find it again. Every day I let it go and it finds me again, and in spite of bouts of negativity and the chronic self-sabotage, I keep seeking those peaks (peeks) of enlightenment.

Thanks for your letter. You have yet to fail me for inspiration. I thank you and am grateful. And I like your dry sense of humor. Keep your head up. Mothers will be mothers.

So, about this new guy at work. I would have to recommend engaging him in some social activity, such as a beer after work sometime, and using that to "get to know" him a little better. Then, using the skills and intellect you possess, decide if you would be offending or pleasing him by actually asking him out.

Have you moved yet? It sounds real nice. Expensive? It will be YOUR space. I wouldn't be surprised at all if you felt somewhat stagnated living where you were. There are of course some past experiences that keep reminding you of stuff there. Isn't that where you and your ex lived before Jen moved in?

ATTENTION EVERYONE: Marcus Ortega now entering a new phase of Life. News at Five.

You Go Boy!! Stay hip.
JT

10.
Hey JT,

I am definitely climbing the mountain within myself: through being extremely depressed for the last week about not being in love (thanks for the reminder).

I sat down in the park on a beautiful evening in October just before sundown and wrote about my realizations, which I am obliged to include in this letter:

[Almost halfway to fifty and finally an undergrad on the horizon, something has clicked inside me like a timer has suddenly expired from one weekend of wild drinking, the bells in my ears heard for miles like a wild church-bell tune. That timer was wound for 18 years, throughout the parental upbringing, until the crying yet joy-filled day I left home to begin my life as a college student. That was the day the clock stopped being wound and was left alone to tick and tock, counting down the days until I realized my party-times should begin to diminish.

"I love drinking" was heard over a drunk-filled neighborhood bar too early in the day to be drowned out by the screeches of the almost-every-night bar fight. A confession of intemperance brought laughs from friends but tears to my soul. The ringing of the alarm clock pounded my entire body for days after this sequence, signaling my need for peace.

Signing a new lease, ridding myself from the never-ending noise of video games, the constant cries of the cats, one wanting out like myself, the other growling to be left alone, again like myself. Beautiful sunsets are becoming more beautiful. Autumn leaves glow brighter. The sounds of wandering branches in the wind as they brush other limbs, removing the last of the summer's breath, those dying leaves falling to their winter home are enhanced to form a perfect spiritual song of rebirth.

I must too be reborn out of this drunk-walk I've stumbled into. All sounds are sent from our God, that great ball of constant flowing energy. Not "God," but the Oversoul, the Universe, the One, all things and non-things. The Source. So the ringing in my head comes also from that source. Fill me with your love so I can feel the reality of my oneness with you. It is necessary for me to forget my yearning for love at this point and feel the comfort within me, the contentment with where my life is leading me, with no remorse, no regret for things I've done or haven't done—no more anger within myself for not saying things or doing things because of a learned fear of being mocked and ridiculed.

Humility is an extremely well liked aspect of a personality; therefore, I should welcome mocking because it builds character. I must only remember that ridiculous words are only used by others as a way of gaining control. I should let this pass and not attempt to regain that energy lost. Instead I should find my energy from other sources: the trees, grass, vibrations of rocks of all kinds, the songs of birds, the chatter of squirrels, the oceans and the breezes. Only in noticing the beauty of all beings can I be filled with energy and love, for love stems from being filled with the oneness and the beauty of all things, living, breathing and not.]

What do you think, Jack?

I began writing this because I seem to get angry with myself for not doing or saying things that I feel I should. It's like others are in control of me, like I'm a puppet. Is it true that wherever we end up, that's what our destiny was? Do we have a say in that?

44

Any control? Can life be better or worse for us? Are we in Hell already, here on Earth? If God is all love and everything around us, then there will be nothing negative about death, right? Which only means that Hell MUST be here on Earth, in the negativity we experience every day. It MUST be the only answer.

Yes, it was Buddha who said, "Some climb, then stop. Some make it all the way to the top." (Although it would have been a bit more poetic had he said, "Some climb, then stop. Some make it to the top." A bit more rhythm that way, don't you think?)

Anyhow, if this is all true, then it's what we MAKE of our lives, not in doing, but in how it FEELS to us (or both I guess) that tells us whether we are in Hell or in Heaven while here on Earth.

That book on the new translations of Jesus' Aramaic words, the one by Neil Douglas Klotz, has really got me thinking lately. I'd always questioned all that mumbo jumbo in the Old Testament of the Bible. Did you know that some people still look for guidance from even the Old Testament? When I did my Bible studies in the dorms, I was thrilled to talk about Jesus' words to the group because it was all about love, as I remember. But the Old Testament, have you read it? God is one mean dude in that book! I swear Jackson, he was like pissed off all the time, and if you didn't do what he said, you were dead!

And then there is stuff like Deuteronomy 24:1-5. (Got out that old heavy Bible—blew the dust off.) If a husband finds some uncleanness in his wife, he can divorce her. If a second guy finds her unclean (or if he dies), then she is defiled because that is an abomination before the lord. And when a guy gets married, he doesn't have to work for a year, but instead he has to stay home and console his wife during that time.

Really? This is why I couldn't keep attending the CCC group because there are actually people that preach this stuff and even more who believe it. It defies all logic to me. Like if A=B and B=C, then A has to = C, right? Not according to the Bible!

So then I must have Faith, with a Capital F. Like for example, here: Proverbs 30:5 says that every word of God is pure. I've got my dictionary here too, and according to Webster, the word "pure" means "clean and not harmful in any way" or "free from moral fault." So that means that if every word of God is pure, then every word of God is free from moral fault and clean and not harmful in any way, right? Well, nope. Not according to the Bible.

Take Ezekial 14:9 for example: If a prophet was deceived, it was Me, the Lord, who deceived him, and I will destroy him too. Said God.

Oh, and here's one: Deuteronomy 25:5-10. If a brother dies, the surviving brother must marry his widow, and if he doesn't want to, the widow will tell the town elders who will then confront the brother. If the brother still doesn't want to marry the widow, she will get to TAKE OFF ONE OF HIS SANDALS, SPIT IN HIS FACE, AND TELL THE WORLD WHAT HE HAS DONE. He will then be renamed: "The family of the unsandaled."

WHAT?!?

Jack, I'm trying to do right by God. I'm trying to do right by my parents and the people I love, but I tell you I can't figure it all out in my brain. I can't seem to understand what God wants, what my mom wants, and how to please everyone... No wonder I drink a lot! I am seeking my innards, man. I'm seeking me, my Self. I want to know who I am and be who I am supposed to be. I feel like I will only like myself (and love myself) once I am on the right path (spiritually). But I AM a SINNER! I just can't figure out why God would make us sinners and then punish us for being sinners. Doesn't make sense!

By the way, it seems like you're the only one I can say this stuff to (and anything else for that matter). I can tell you about my partying, about my love interests, about my writing and my family, and my thoughts, and questions about God (not a lot of people will stand for questioning God around here), and anything else, and you just keep writing back and telling me to hang in there. Love you man! I keep wondering though if I'm going to finally say something that pisses you off. Hopefully not.

Okay, I just got back from class. I was sharing what I had just been writing, all the crazy stuff about the Bible, with this guy named Mike in my class. He's got long, hippy hair, is a history major, but takes a lot of lit classes. He just bathes in the stuff. I was telling him about all the contradictions in the Old Testament, and he said it wasn't just the Old Testament, it was all over the Bible. Here's one in the New Testament that he pointed me to: 1 John 3: 8-10. If you are born of God, you cannot sin. He that sins is of the devil.

Huh? I thought we were all God's children. I thought we were ALL sinners and must confess our sins to God or Christ in order to have them forgiven. Now they're saying that sinners are not born of God?

Help! I'm going to go have a cigarette and a beer and maybe a bath since it's all going down hill from here.

Okay, no more psycho-babble bullshit. Yes, the dull life of non-thinking red-necked flotation in the world is definitely not for me either! However, I must admit I have found myself slipping into that mode once in a while. You just can't seem to avoid them, really, which gets me thinking... maybe they're confused as to what to do, who to please, and how to make God happy too, so then they just throw their arms up in the air and have a cigarette, a beer, and a bath... Just a thought.

Take care and talk at you soon. By the way, Transcendentalism: the belief in a higher power connecting all things (God, but NOT God). Oversoul, they call it. It stresses individualism (Emerson), vegetarianism (Thoreau), and calmness filled with love of all things.

Ciao.
Marc

11.
Marco!

It is good to hear from you. Good to hear you are doing well (I think). I am especially glad to hear the things you wrote about wanting to find love within and for yourself. You can't give what you don't have. Self love does not have to be egotism. It seems weird, but I think you and I are going through some similar phases of change, ie. trying to correct & modify those feelings of anger toward ourselves by doing what WE want. Not doing something because someone else wants us to. Someone said, not sure I remember who, that failure is not about making the wrong turn. It's about staying on the wrong path as if it's the only route. Who is anyone else to tell you who you are and where you should go and what you should do in your life anyways?

I'm beginning to look at it this way: I am me, right? And you are you, no? And my friend Christy is, well, Christy, right? What pleases me pleases me, and not necessarily you or Christy. Remember when we were on our trip, and you stuck with your beer and cigarettes while I partook in some sweet nature's nectar? I think I maybe asked you twice, and then realized you didn't like it. I didn't force you to do it, and you (and good for you) didn't do it just to please me.

So why do we feel the need to do things just to please others? And yet a better question is why are others still trying to control us? You love who you love, and I enjoy a bit of S&M now and then (just to get my point across).

As a result of thinking this way, I'm gaining more self-respect, confidence. (I'm feeling like I should get a tattoo in your honor!)

Make peace with the natural world, including the nature of our selves. I've learned that loving someone and being in love with someone are two very different things. I can now see that they are different in regards to the self as well. I am not IN love with myself (conceit, egotism), but I do love myself (self respect, dignity, integrity). Do you feel that way about yourself?

I hear you on the Bible contradictions. They go on and on. I wrote an essay on the Bible once attempting to compare and contrast God's love versus his anger. Not sure how well I did. The prof thought it was good, an "interesting examination of the nature of good and evil," she said, but the peer editing didn't go so well. Maybe we'll look it over when you get to town next.

By the way, I don't think we ever talked about you having Bible studies in the dorms. It seemed, on our trip, that the numerous references to God and the afterlife were of "the One," or "the Oversoul," and "returning to that eternal energy that pervades the universe." I remember you saying something about Campus Crusade for Christ, but in your letter, it sounds as though you "led" or "taught" Bible studies? Tell me more.

I have to say, Marc, in all sincerity, I am inspired and enlightened by different parts in all your letters. I truly enjoy our communication. When are you coming to visit?

Meaningful coincidence: I picked up a couple of small essay books at a bookstore on Fourth Avenue a couple days before I received your letter (now that I think about it, it would have probably been when you were <u>writing</u> the letter. Wow). I got the essay *Nature* by Ralph Waldo Emerson and *Walking* by Thoreau. Wild, wacky, stuff. I dig the transcendental stuff. Transcendental realism = my religion.

I <u>very much</u> enjoyed your self-affirming writing (the photocopied pages). Very much. I had a similar experience in the desert a week or so ago:

[I've wandered out to let the desert be my friend. As hostile and uninviting as it may seem, it can really be peace and beauty if you hold it right. Prickly saguaro, mesquite javelina, and roadrunners. I hope this dream will last.

Quail flutter as doves sit nearby, cooing while something like a whippoorwill calls its mate. Close by, flies buzz my head as patrolmen scout for vandals alongside lonely coyotes. Quail chirp their conversation and take barely a notice, so it seems, to my presence. I hear the planes overhead, but when I look up all I see are peaks and points of the Santa Catalinas.

There are browns of wood, dark and deep, by the stone I sit on. Vibrant greens and reds, yellows embedded in my perception before me. Barrel cactus and ragweed type plants along with some sort of pear cactus all define and embody the rugged life surrounding me. Left alone to be with my self, I sit, absorb, become part of the desert. Open up around me, pull me in and make me yours, if only for a little while.

I live in a desert but survive in the city. Work, eat, sleep with but a few scattered reminders that the wilderness exists thriving around me and full of itself. Far too often do I not visit the solitude about me. Instead I hibernate stoned in my den of MTV and Comedy Central (both of which only occasionally entertain or enlighten me). I watch Willie Nelson's "Live at the Texas Opry House" and Neil Young's "Rust Never Sleeps" almost every day. Singing, writing, thinking, learning about myself and everyone else. Simply glad to be free again. Free in a relative sense, but free nonetheless to do what I wish, go where I want. People send me letters and call on the phone, telling me they miss me. I miss them too, but I had to leave. I had to live. I was dying up there.

Now the fresh air captivates me, fills me with renewal and empowerment. I am now in full control, of my choices, of my actions. Responsible, I live again. Alive again. I grow, again.]

So anyway, that was my little meditative desert experience. I have since then been back out there a couple of times. It's a place called Sabino Canyon. Very beautiful. Very relaxing.

Well, I suppose this is enough of an opus. I leave you with a few haiku:

Sit closer darlin'
Let me feel the warmth of your eyes
The depth of your soul

Don't bother me now
I am trying to open
Minds up to the world

Anyhow, I hope you have a good day. Every day is a good day. Take it easy. Write.
Jackson

12.
Señor Jackson,

Well I'm into my new place. I've been swarmed with a mess of trash and boxes of shit stacked high. Shit unused for years, hauled place to place, extra work for no satisfaction. And like the boy bees, I've bowed to the Lux Queen 12 of the last 14 days. But now, my Sabbath, a day of rest, a smokey treat, a cup of java, and a look at your latest letter. I've been reminded lately that all things in our world revolve around money. Even Thoreau, upon retreating into the woods, discovered he'd need some money to build his small cabin and to eat.

Yep, I was the Bible study guy the first half of my sophomore year in the dorms. Seems so long ago. I only led like one and a half "levels." I think I started the second level group, but only a couple guys came the first night and then it just sputtered out. Was trying to find myself, man (still am?). I was working on my internal feelings, you know! Shortly after though, I started giving in to my "unclean" sexual desires...and I guess it felt so good that I stopped attending the CCC meetings. (Actually, I began to see hypocrisy and bigotry in the group, so I quit.) I began to think that all that stuff in the Bible was meant to scare and thus control people. It's easier to control people by saying you'd kill them (or they won't receive the kingdom of God) than by saying "do this because I love you." Do you think the church wrote all that stuff about God's wrath in the Bible just to gain control over the people?

I've been thinking about that a lot lately, and about money. Since money rules the world, I'm thinking that the church felt that the more money they had, the more control they would have. That's why they say you need to put like ten percent of your paycheck into the coffers. That's probably also why they wrote that homosexuality is bad, since they needed the earth to be populated in order to boost the church's income—not a lot of kids being born of homosexual sex. Did you know that some Native American cultures believed (still do, I think...) that homosexuals were half God? Interesting.

By the way, I love what you wrote, that failure is not in making a wrong turn, but staying on the wrong path as if it were the only route. Beautifully stated. You seem to always know what you're talking about. Be sure that tat in honor of me is of a big penis. Just kidding. Make it an OM or something.

It would be nice to have a desert prairie nearby to which I could retreat for clarity. I suppose, for the meantime, I could create something in my own mind and retreat there now and then.

I bought a new book by Marc Hammer called *The Jeshua Letters*. He apparently wrote it while streaming the Oversoul. Interesting! Believable? I tell you what though, it was a very quick read, and I just knew after finishing it that I had lived the life of Jesus, just like you and everyone else has, and that we're all connected and have been and will be for all of eternity. I KNEW it!

But it always fades as the clock ticks on. I need to keep reading, reminding.

Did I tell you I went as Sinead O'rtega for Halloween? Yep, shaved the head, and I've got to tell you, I've never before experienced such blatant

stereotyping based on physical appearance before
(toward myself that is—I've seen it happen to
others—my Korean friend Kevin, for example—
apparently my mixed Chilean skin makes me look
more white than exotic—and English is my first
language anyway).

Anyhow, twice at Sisters Sports Bar and once at
Winners (where I was only hanging out to humor
friends), I was shoved by big white guys. Never
before had I been pushed around like this until I
shaved the head, so it couldn't have been a
coincidence. Stereotyping is sad, but at least, on the
bright side, the anger was toward what these guys
perceived as being a skinheaded white-pride guy.
But, nope, just Sinead O'rtega.

I love my new pad. Finally had a chance to throw
about 6 boxes of shit out that I don't want to haul
around anymore. I used the disposal for the first
time today on some 1-cup o' vegetarian chili that
totally sucked—yuck.

No poetry lately. Racing around to school and work
has extinguished the pilot light in my mind (and
heart and soul at times). Hopefully a couple days off
and a cup of Indian Love Tea will help it to kindle
yet again. The breath of God is in all things of this
universe (regardless of whether or not Jesus is
involved—yes, I need to keep reminding myself of
this).

Peace bro!
Marc

13.
Marco Marc.

Que Pasa? Lux Queen is making you work hard for her, huh? Bitch. All good I hope.

Just a quick note. Most everything is good here. My job is going well—got four 10-hour shifts so I get Wednesdays, Thursdays, and Sundays off. I like it. I get to interact with the kids more, and I'm learning every day.

I picked up some <u>more</u> new music (new to my collection). I know, I spend a little too much on music sometimes. O-well. Music and books get more of my cash these days than drugs or alcohol so I don't feel that bad about it. I got the new Smashing Pumpkins double disc set, good if you like the Pumpkins. I also got a Stone Temple Pilots disc and some Ani DiFranco. You would love Ani. I HIGHLY RECOMMEND you make some of her music one of your very next musical priorities. She's folk/punk, if you can imagine that. <u>Quite</u> good. I also got a Lou Reed/John Cale disc which is a tribute to Andy Warhol. They were both in the Velvet Underground. It's called *Songs For Drella*.

Isn't realizing expectation is like a prison liberating?! I find it so. When I find myself waiting or expecting something, I can realize how futile and counterproductive it so often is. Just let whatever happen and enjoy all moments from beginning to end without undo mental stress placed upon oneself by expectation. Let it flow. Let it go.

So how is snow country with no hair? It sucks to hear you got harassed, but I enjoyed your ability to see the bright side.

The breath of God is in all things of this earth... Yes, the creative forces that brought about this world, this configuration of all things living and inanimate, exist within each and every bit, every atom of energy, every electron that jumps orbit. These forces are incomprehensible and shall remain that way.

Speaking of it (love), I've spent a fair amount of time lately thinking about love and relationships, well, more particularly, Love. It is enigmatic and as large as life, way too unsolvable to spend too much time on. Nowadays I just try to figure out what I feel inside and often come up with love of different levels. Different kinds of love coexist within different and the same relationships. Leo Buscaglia wrote a good book on love. It's called *Love*. It is not long; pick it up some day. I haven't read it in 4 years, but I remember it opened up a lot of shudders and let a lot of light in.

A couple words about money: it's NOT the root of all evil, as the church wants everyone to think. (You actually WILL make it into "heaven" regardless of how rich you are—everyone does.) But it CAN become more important than your fellow human, at which point, I would question its "goodness." But, with money, one can feed the hungry, build shelters for the homeless, create and dispense medicine, etc. (If you can't tell, I'm trying to think kind thoughts about money.) And money can buy a big penis tattoo for my forearm. Or would it look better on my left butt cheek?

Cultivate Patience
Grow Understanding
Truth is Simplicity.

–JT

14.
Hey JT,

My Hell week at school is over, and I'm pretty much free until after Thanksgiving. I walked up to Red Oak tonight and ordered Emerson's *Nature,* then to Deaf Ear to order Ani DiFranco's latest. You know me well enough. I'm sure I can trust your judgment.

I met that history major guy I was talking about for a beer at the Eagle's Nest after class today. (Remember the Eagle's Nest? Our old stomping, thinking, drinking, brainstorming ground?). Anyhow, he was telling me about a discussion he had in a class today about how the old textbooks used to say things like, "The Indians, at the time the Europeans came, were aggressive warriors who slaughtered many white people." Interesting, huh? Notice the heavy slanting with the words "aggressive" and "slaughtered." Apparently the textbooks were riddled with stuff like this, opinionated propaganda. I think the Bible was written like that too. My mom says that the Bible tells us how we can spot another Christian so we know those we should convene with. I hope they're not all as vindictive as God is in the Old Testament... What do you think?

I wanted to comment on your comments about money really quick. It's fucked up to me how the church wants people to think money is evil, and then they want each member of their congregations to give a chunk of their money to them. And it's funny how they do it too. If you <u>don't</u> give us your money, then you're not doing your part, and if you're not doing your part, we are not going to be able to help you to get your sins forgiven by God so then you're going to Hell, right? Oh, and those of you giving money to us, thanks, but if you don't stop with those unclean thoughts already (Hey, I saw you, Mr. Johnson, looking at Mr. Murphy's wife—that's adultery), then you're not going to make it to Heaven anyhow.

It's like they purposely breed the fear in order to create this cycle of dependency—on them—then you'll have to continue to give them their fair chunk of your paycheck. AND, you feel like shit about yourself because you can't change a behavior (you drink too much) or you can't stop thinking about your neighbor's wife (or husband), and it's just this continuous cycle of negativity, and you continue to feel bad about yourself and keep coming back to church in order to be forgiven and try to feel good about yourself again, but then... It's never-ending!

Oh my God! THEY'RE GENIUSES!

They've got it all figured out! Create the cycle and it keeps the money flowing. And the worst part, now that I think about it, is they're tax-free! They don't pay a dime to the government (or, therefore, to the people for that matter) because they are non-profit, tax-exempt (whatever) "entities."

So, the church creates this cycle of negativity, of dependency, which brings THEM money, yet the people feel so bad about themselves that oftentimes they get pulled into alcoholism or drug use and then can't hold down a job or get sick or try killing themselves—all of which costs the government and the people money, interestingly. Yet the church is making a buttload!

Like I said, GENIUSES!

I'm heading downtown to get drunk. It's Friday night, and I've got to wash the guilt of these unclean thoughts away (including the one of a giant penis on your left butt cheek.)

Talk to you soon, Brother Jackson.
Marc.

KJV: "Blessed are they which are persecuted for righteousness' sake for theirs is the kingdom of heaven."

Other translation: "Aligned with the One are those who draw shame for their pursuit of natural stability; theirs is the ruling principle of the cosmos"

OR "their new home is the province of the universe" (Klotz 68).

HMMM. ONE ENERGY, don't you think?
Marc

15.
Marco,

Selling point for homosexuality according to T.V.'s Seinfeld: If you date someone your size, you instantly double your wardrobe.

Just one of many I am sure. Whatever that means.

Well, I've gone ahead and done it. I am taking control of my life and my body. This is ME and this is MINE, damn it! I've gotten a tattoo in your honor. I'll show it to you sometime.

I'm at work right now. Quiet house—boys asleep, sound and warm. Me awake, trying to stay cool to stay awake. This vigil is often a challenge to my conscious determination to retain wakefulness. I usually do well though. I have a movie *Taxi Driver* with Robert De Niro, Jodie Foster, and Cybill Shepard. It is supposed to be a very powerful film. 1970's. Scorsese. Last night I watched *The Fisher King*. That's a good movie too. If you haven't seen it, I would recommend it.

I found a book at the library to read as well (as I inevitably get tired of staring at the tube), another Paulo Coehlo book. It's called *The Valkyries*.

Apparently it's about angels and such. I'm not too much into angels, but I liked *The Alchemist* so I thought I'd give it a shot.

Next week for work I go to a "training" of some kind for "bad kids." I guess these kids would just as soon kill you as shake your hand. It is supposedly at a real delinquent's school. We'll see how it goes. Hopefully it will be a truly enlightening experience. If it doesn't prove to be exciting, I'll be bummin' (I've got it for 3 days, 8 hours a day.)

I'm glad you are still going to the Eagle's Nest. That place was pretty much ours, a hidden gem that the meatheads ignored.

About the Bible. I think they HAD to write it like that. Remember, in Biblical times, there were sacrifices, wars everywhere, every-man-for-himself kind of craziness (and women had NO power at all!). The easiest way to stop all that was to create fear in people—if you do it, you'll die. God (the Gods) will come and strike you down. But the problem now is that the Bible still exists as law. Even though humans have changed (evolved) significantly, religion seems to stay stagnant. (Is this why so many of us continue to search and search...?)

Imagine if we still wrote on stone tablets even though someone was smart enough to come up with paper. Or imagine if we still denied the fact that the world is round or still held on to the notion that Earth is the center of the universe. The world needs to continue to encourage the courageous, those who will take the next step without fear to explore new ideas and (again without fear) to report their findings. And we are doing that, my man. We are on the road (again).

Tell me more about your experience with Campus Crusade for Christ. I knew a girl, Kate, who went to those "meetings." I remember her saying she really liked going. She went to some prayer groups too. She loved those.

Well, I'm sort of getting tired now. I took a break and watched *Taxi Driver*. I could see how it would have been more powerful back when it came out. I think by now though, compared to movies like *Pulp Fiction*, it isn't all that shocking. It was good though.

It's 4:41 AM. Boys start to get up in 2-3 hours. Hope everything's going well for you. I bet it's cold up there.

Until next time,
Jack

16.
Hello Sir,

Interesting, standing at Red Oak Books, chatting with a friend, she was telling me about an experience she had during a certain type of meditation seminar (I forgot what it was called). She actually saw something inside herself which was the answer to a question held by someone else in the group whom she didn't know—she didn't know the question either (one energy, no?).

At this point, I was at the height of my energy-filled feelings on this brisk, sunny November day. Resting on one foot, I began to wobble a bit, then started to lean, and when I caught myself, I found myself staring at a book on the shelf—it just caught me, out of the blue. *The Valkyries*. Now, this was on a Monday (I bought the book by the way), and I received your letter on Thursday, which told me about this new book about Angels that you'd found, called, yep, *The Valkyries*. I think we're connected, man! I haven't read much yet, but it seems to be about much more than just angels (to your delight, most likely). It seems to be Universal—Energetic. I'm only 25 pages in, and already there is mention of rocks, plants, animals, and humans all having different types of a universal energy.

Yes, I agree with the doubling of the wardrobe when you start dating someone your size, and I have in the past. The problem is I'm sort of a lesbian when it comes to choosing wears. I despise many gay men's wardrobes—often too tight and too flashy. Yuck!

My CCC (Campus Crusade) experience, for the most part, up until I had some friends who "didn't fit in" to the group, was excellent. I remember feeling so welcomed, so loved, so accepted, at first. People were just nice, never trying to one-up you or tease, ridicule, or put you down for any reason, at first. They never talked about you behind your back, got too drunk to remember the bad things they had said

65

about you (never drank actually), and they seemed to always want to help, at first.

Then, showing signs of questioning the whole "faith" aspect, like really wanting to understand the WHY's (you know how I am), I found myself not being called for a prayer group (those WERE wonderful by the way), or feeling alone at a meeting. (I like your quotes around "meeting" in your letter. Correct, they were actually often "presentations" or "preaching sessions"—sermons, etc.).

So, all in all, I enjoyed all the things the CCC group had to offer except the judgment. It's funny how lesson after lesson in the Bible studies focused on Jesus helping this, that, and the other unfortunate person, but then in real life, people find excuses to just ditch those who are not of the norm. It's like they don't want to be "stained" by their unrighteousness or something.

On to more positive things: poetry. Have I told you that I absolutely LOVE your haiku:

Don't bother me now
I am trying to open
Minds up to the world.

It's funny. It's like we're tied together on the same wavelength, like you're answering my questions before I ask them, like you just know, somewhere inside, all the mucky stuff inside me and are tossing out the mineral spirits that will wash them away.

In this, your fantastic haiku poem, the "I" character is basically shutting the door on those people seeking him/her out instead of letting them in and helping them to open their minds. It's a statement on how all (many) beings, who believe they have open minds, often treat others, by shutting them out. It's like how the CCC group made me feel, seriously. (Although I can seriously understand not wanting to be around all the negativity that judgmental people harbor.)

One time, during prayer group in the basement of my dorm, Luke, one of the RA's, poked his head into the room looking for a student. The group sort of stopped praying for a moment after that (I think we were all surprised when Luke came in), but one of the girls in the group ended up starting to cry. She got all upset and started complaining about how people can't read and respect a simple sign on a door: "Prayer group in session. Please do not disturb."

It's funny, this subject of prayer. What do many prayers consist of? Something similar to, "Lord Jesus, please help [so and so] to see the light...feel your love...come to you...let salvation rest in them...protect them from danger/evil..." In essence, they are trying to open minds up to the world [to God, perhaps] or they're trying to open other minds so that the individual person/people they are praying for will be protected. However, in doing so, they shut out all other "nuisances" or seem to be bothered by any type of interruption. Sort of like,

"Hey, open your mind, but you there, get out of here—you're bugging us..."

I guess what I'm trying to say is that you've got a pretty damn good little haiku there.

You go guy! I believe I will have another.

I have to mention this. When I look back on these prayer groups, I have some giddy, yummy, nice feelings about them. They felt good. It was like we were helping, or trying to help. But I've also got this nagging feeling, like if someone prayed for me to do something, or feel a certain way, or see the light, and it went completely against everything I believe, I would get pissed. Who gives anybody in this world the authority to say this is right for you and that is wrong for you. It's almost like they are trying to strip away my free will, the very essence of what makes me Me.

By the way, I'm looking forward to seeing your penis. I hope it's healing up nicely.

Let's see, I've got a beer date after work tomorrow night with a twenty-three year old UW-Madison graduate (philosophy)—should be interesting—conversation-wise—and don't-know-if-he's-straight-or-gay-wise. Hmmm. Then a coffee date this weekend with a guy in one of my classes—smart (very smart), interesting, cute, vegan, although another question mark on the sexual preference issue. I don't know why I keep getting myself into this mucky sort of water... Oh well, I'll find out sooner... I go guy! Boy, this filled-with-energy coincidence stuff is pretty cool! It's confidence boosting, I am ME sort of fun! Lovin' it! Of course Ma would say I am living for this world rather than for Jesus, fun hater that she is.

I had this daydream of you. I could see you...in a beautiful wooden chair, leaning back, legs crossed, pipe in one hand, reading glasses perhaps, and a cup of tea. You are lecturing on the psychology of cult phenomena, applause from a captivated audience of graduate students and mentors...

Love it. Three weeks of classes left. Yee hah, country. Gotta go; the drinkin' buddies are arriving.

Peace Brother.
Marc.

17.
My Brother, My Brother:

It is good to hear from you again. It sounds as if you are doing well and are content with life.

Thanksgiving was good. Jess & I cleaned house, drank several Bloody Mary's (with Becks chasers) and smoked some good tobacco. It was a good day of meditative relaxation to remember what I am thankful for and what I appreciate. A good day.

I've been rather melancholy, however, the last day or two. I think it's a combination of Thanksgiving Day reflection and everything that was smoked in the process. I don't necessarily feel depressed, just sort of calm. Like the top of the water.

I loved your rampage about the church and money and control and fear. I feel it man!

Are you thinking of coming down? It sounds like Jess has a few La Crosse friends talking about coming down sometime too. It will be interesting to see what January looks like/brings. Man, I sincerely do hope you come and visit. I need a renewal in my inspiration. I am sick of writing love poems—they seem to turn out so bitter these days—and I need to have a creative/inspiring encounter. Who knows, maybe the holiday season in the desert will spur some new thoughts to the surface. But I'd still like to see you come down.

Yes, my new tattoo has healed nicely, although I must inform you that I chose to forgo the penis. Sorry to let you down. I did, however, get the yin/yang on my left butt cheek (well, just below the waistline actually).

Take care, mi amigo.
JT

18.
Jack,

Yes, I am SO looking forward to seeing your left butt cheek. A Yin/Yang in my honor? Am I all up and down on you, darkness and light? I am hoping to head through Arizona and stop for a visit on my way out to California. Yes, California!

Update: Marc's cousin's employer has offered Marc a position in a casting agency beginning ASAP. Don't quite know what it entails, but I've accepted the job for the meantime. We'll see if I like it or not— at least it will get me where I want to be—West, San Diego to be exact (a bit further west than I had expected, but...). Last day of employment in La Crosse, Wisconsin: December 25. Gee, Tucson's right on the way.

School's fine. A little stressful, but that's expected at the end of the semester. Excitement is mounting.

I met a young man on the train from Milwaukee to La Crosse last Friday. He was heading to a pipe-laying job in the cities from New Orleans. Half Italian, he had quite the interesting and exotic accent and a deep, effective voice. A gentle man who has had quite the hard life. As an example, he showed me a stab wound on his chest...nice chest. What intrigued and inspired me about this 23 year old man was his vigor and love—pure love and excitement for life, regardless of his difficult upbringing in the schools of New Orleans.

I tell you what man, it seems next to impossible to cross paths these days with someone who holds the same views and love for living, nature, and people as you and me. Talk about coincidences! It was interesting how we met: I got on the train in Milwaukee and only had a choice of sitting next to someone, since there was no two-seat section open. I walked all the way to the front of the car, my mind picking and choosing, weighing each option the entire time. Finally, I just said screw it and sat in a seat with a black leather coat next to it. Walt came back and sat down after about 20 minutes, and five minutes later we were in the lounge car smoking cigarettes, drinking beer, and having a grand old time. Weird, huh? I just noticed, as I'm writing this, that his name is WALT! Like Walt Whitman, transcendental, nature, love yourself, love life, the One, you are me and I am you, you know…

The Celestine Prophecy suggests that the coincidences will happen if we are filled with the natural and universal good energy. I guess we are filled, my friend. Yee Haa Desert Bumkin!

I have shared your haiku with my poetry classes. Great responses.

Dating scene in La Crosse is slow, but I believe that since I am leaving sooner than expected, the dating thing will have to wait. Oh well, I think I can cope. By the way, I believe I too am in need of some inspiring company as yourself. Walt was cool and all, but we've got ROOTS, you and me. I will phone you as soon as I know the dates.

CHEAP FUN IS GOOD! LOVE POEMS <u>CAN</u> SUCK!

Jot soon, Bud.
Love ya.
Marc.

P.S. New UW-L literary magazine is named after a word used in one of my poems... Steamticket (that's mine). A Third Coast Review... Ponder that!

19.
Mr. Ortega.

Congrats. Congrats. Congrats. I have heard both pros and cons about San Diego. I will have to come check it out personally sometime (when I come to visit??).

Yes we are all Yin/Yang, and it is actually (I believe) the Yin that drives the Yang, the negative helps us to see what we don't want or what doesn't feel good which then helps us to produce more of the positive or that which we want. Most people choose to give up, or throw their arms into the air like Joe Redneck, because they don't understand the process (or have the energy/desire to deal with it). But I think if we are consciously aware of the Yin, we can then consciously choose to move more toward the Yang. I'm now thinking I should have gotten my tattoo on my forearm instead of my butt cheek to serve as a constant reminder to me to move consciously through life every minute of the day. O, I guess I'll have to consider another tat. They are addicting.

Jessie and I are looking for a new apartment. What a pain! O well. So anyway, by the time you swing on through, we'll actually have some space to let you sleep. Cool.

73

I was talking to an old friend from La Crosse, another Psych major, and she turned me on to Joseph Campbell. Like a breath of fresh air! Have you read anything by him? It's all Mythology and archetypes and how it relates to our present culture (and its confusion). Very cool stuff. I am reading *The Power of Myth,* but I guess his other works are good too, esp. *The Hero With a Thousand Faces.*

One concept he put forth, that might grasp your attention, is that of dreams being private myths and myths being public dreams. Also to the movie *Star Wars* as the newest public idealization (myth). Very cool stuff.

Concerning your man from New Orleans, I had a comic flash regarding commentary on his job as a pipe-layer (i.e. a little pipe laying job of your own) but since I have such good taste, I won't get into it…

Hey, I FINALLY got something half-assed to come out of my melon. It's a song that I wrote last week in a key of C with a C, F, C, F (slide) 6 progression. It's tentatively called "Soulmate Companion" and is about just that. Not that it will be performed for any sort of audience, just for personal expression. But hey, isn't that what IT is about?

Coincidences kick ass, don't they. Yes they do. I think they happen all the time. But only when one is more filled with the (+) positive energy of life than with the (-) negative energy does one realize or see the occurrence of these coincidences to their fullest potential. The positive energy allows for better positive vision, sheds light on more of the opportunities of life than the downfalls. Make any sense? Or you could look at it as the positive being connected with the life force, and the negative being that of man-made self-doubt and ego. Isn't it Buddha who said the ego is a myth of the self?

Another good book I am reading, that coincidentally ties in very well with the mythical forum, is *Black Elk Speaks* by John G. Neihardt. It is the (essentially) life account of a Sioux shaman. I tell you, just trying to imagine the experience of his "vision" is tremendous. The detail is amazing. Very informative literature, sociologically, anthropologically, culturally, historically, and psychologically.

We are filled, my friend. Yes, one energy. I sure do miss the Eagle's Nest Daze as well. Those are some shining flecks (nuggets) of gold in a year consisting of many lumps of lead. Definitely.

Marc Ortega is the SHIT! UW-L literati know their stuff (at least as far as publication titles go). Although I'm not sure of the meaning, it does sound cool.

Well, I'll be anticipating a call from you sometime in the next few weeks. If no one is home, the answering machine will pick up. It is Gloria's voice so don't be alarmed.

Take care of yourself.
Peace and Love,
Jack.

20.
Jackson,

Upon first viewing a paper returned from my Shakespeare teacher, I read: "Marc, could you make me a copy?" I immediately knew she liked it. Looking at the back page, I read:

> Marc,
> I sit in the only feeding outlet in Kellogg, Minnesota, a small café with juxtaposed modern kitsch and antique carpentry. One of my fellow diners, I learn, is named Clem. Disconsolate because I feel a great sense of failure—failure to quicken, enliven, empower or liberate the learning process for students, I conclude that I must become an automaton, I must act like those machines I so much abhor. And then your paper surfaces on the stack. I read. I read a discussion concerned with benevolence. And I am liberated.

Do you want some energy? Tell you what, I don't need all of it that I've received from one of my most liberating teachers. Professor Cannon is her name. She has <u>always</u> made me think in the two classes I've taken with her, but she has never made me tear up before. I guess I've always been a pretty nice guy, always trying to do right, look out for others, help others. It's just natural to me. I will have to show you the piece. It's kind of neat—very transcendental.

Have I told you before that 3 of the 4 most interesting people I have met recently are vegetarians? Other veg heads include (not that I've met any of <u>these</u> folks): Pythagoras, Socrates, Plato, Aristotle, daVinci, Newton, Voltair, Thoreau, Shaw, Ben Franklin, Edison, Albert Schweitzer, and Gandhi! Pretty good list, huh? Not that I'm promoting it (well actually I guess I kind of am), but somebody mentioned that when animals are butchered, they're so filled with fear and anger, and the chemicals associated with those emotions race through every muscle and cell in their bodies (kind of like a huge adrenaline rush or how it feels when you're so afraid you can't move you legs—fight, flight, or freeze). Those chemicals are the same as those in the human body that cause the emotions of fear and anger. When we eat the flesh from animals killed in that way, we also take in those emotion-causing chemicals—I guess we sort of smell death. Sorry, depressing. It was just a thought. Kind of makes some sense though, huh—maybe?

A week of stress left. Then freedom. The entire world will be mine.

It's interesting how the stress caused by events and deadlines in everyday student life seems to dissipate when I focus my energy on writing a letter to you. And I must thank you for being one of the very few people (the only one?) that I can say/write absolutely anything to and not feel stupid—thanks for listening.

Well, the folks (both sets) are going to be here for graduation. Should be interesting. Then right after Christmas, I'm off to San Diego. I think I am going to be very sad, but Mary Jane says I shouldn't censor my tears so if they flow, I'm gonna let them! I'll probably be too excited about my new start to even recognize any sadness until I'm about halfway there.

UPDATE: My cousin quit her job at the casting agency. I guess the guy wasn't paying her. So I'm 86 a job right now, but who cares. I'm not going to let that bother me. I still feel something overwhelmingly compelling me to go.

Talk to you soon.
Love, your astral brother.
Marc.

I am unsure of everything that happened in between Christmas and Marc's arriving in San Diego. The letters don't say much; there may be one or two missing. In the letters leading up to Marc's move, he had anticipated visiting Jackson in Tucson on his way out to California, but that didn't happen. Nor did Marc write to Jack to tell him exactly why, though there are a couple brief references in later letters to a lack of car insurance.

Marc's graduation had finally arrived. He was a couple years older than his classmates and a few years older than Jack, although Marc often thought that Jack seemed a few steps ahead of him in the arena of book-smarts. (Future letters from Jack would reveal his disdain for his 18 years behind the bars of the public education system.)

Marc had taken a couple years off before his undergrad years. He traveled the country, selling aerial photos to farmers and ranchers and meeting people who helped him expand his understanding of humanity. That sales job took him throughout Pennsylvania, Ohio, Iowa, Illinois, Wisconsin, Minnesota, Nebraska, Colorado, Utah, Nevada, and California. All this travel actually proved helpful for his overall grade point average; he felt much more street-smart, more experienced in life than many of his classmates seemed. So, for Marc, graduation was like lifting a burden from him, like uncovering a precious stone.

On graduation day, he was clearly a bit fuzzy. Both sets of parents were there, his mom and stepdad Paul, and his dad and stepmom Maria. His mom and dad didn't get along the greatest—not that they fought or anything, they just didn't have much to talk about. Marc hadn't seen them together since his brother's wedding a few years prior.

That was the night his mom found out Marc was gay and cornered him in the men's bathroom, saying, "How dare you turn this celebration into a focus on you!"

Marc had brought his boyfriend Nathan to the wedding under the guise of him being just a friend. Only his father and stepmother knew he was gay at the time. He had tried to tell his brother once about a year or so prior, but his brother, Ben, popped the fact that he was going to be a father first so Marc didn't want to spoil the moment for him.

"What was it you wanted to tell me?" Ben asked after they celebrated his news for a moment with a couple swallows of beer.

"Well," Marc stumbled. "I've already got two kids," he joked. Ben about spit up his beer as Marc rumbled with laughter. And with that they moved on to other subjects.

Back at Ben's wedding, their mother was trying to make it an issue and blame it all on Marc.

"How am I making the focus on me?" he jabbed, standing his ground.

"I know Nathan's your boyfriend. Why would you do this, bringing your gay boyfriend to a family event?"

Marc just walked out—he'd never been one for confrontations.

She'd done this before, though not to Marc. She'd done this to his sister several times, once blaming her behavior for their mom and dad's divorce. She'd done it to Marc's brother as well, when he was in high school, tracking him down at a friend's house and blaming him for their stepdad's anger.

"Fuck you," Ben hollered at her, then ran from his friend's house, not headed in the direction of home.

At least Marc had just walked away from her at the wedding. He didn't scream out "fuck you" like his brother had, although he had wanted to.

Marc went to Ben immediately, and thinking the buzz had spread throughout the whole room, the entire wedding party, and all the guests, he apologized to his brother for bringing Nathan. Ben sort of just shook a "whatever" response and then kept dancing. So it was done.

But geez, *I'm not even safe in the men's bathroom,* thought Marc.

A few months later, Nathan and Marc took a motorcycle trip to Iowa to visit Ben and his new wife who accepted them as boyfriends with open arms. The brothers shared their moody mother stories, and somewhere inside, they both knew that wouldn't be the end of them.

Needless to say, getting himself ready on graduation morning took Marc a little extra time. He made sure to sit and breathe for a few minutes, to look in the mirror and remind himself that he loves his mom, no matter how difficult she could be. It's no wonder there was heavy drinking the night before!

The two ended up being respectful of each other, although his dad and Maria were a bit guarded due to Marc's mom being there (she was always a good guilt-tripper—see above). Marc joined his dad and Maria for lunch since they had planned to drive back to Milwaukee that same day, and he planned to meet his mom and Paul, who had reserved a hotel room for the night, for dinner that evening.

At the restaurant for dinner—they went to Marc's favorite place, Fayzees—Paul slipped Marc a fifty dollar bill and joined him at the bar for a scotch and water and a cigarette. "Don't tell your mother," said Paul, as usual.

Dinner was fine; in public it usually was. After dinner, Paul retired to the hotel, and Marc asked his mom if she'd like to see his apartment. They'd been getting along fine, and Marc was proud of his solo living for the first time. She agreed, and they walked from the hotel to Marc's apartment and had a nice visit for about the first 8 and a half minutes.

Marc could feel the uneasiness set in; his mother looked down at the island counter, picked up a piece of junk mail, fiddled with it quietly for a moment, then flipped it over pretending to read the back.

"You know it's not right," she started. With Marc's mom, it was always like this. He'd think they're having a nice time and then POW. "It's just not natural, Marcus. God didn't intend for men to be sleeping with other men. And to go advertising it all over, my goodness."

Marc felt he needed to close the drapes over the pictures on the walls, if only there were any. He had thought they were quite classy—no nudity, nothing obvious, just men in thought, pondering the death of a loved one, or their own oppression, perhaps. He felt exposed, more naked than ever before.

They cried, eventually. She had won again, as usual.

Marc spent the next few days trying to lift his head up, complaining to his father about her. His father was always supportive, for the most part.

"Ah don know why you poot yourself troo dat," his dad would say jokingly, in his heavy Chilean accent, trying to lift his son's spirits. "Eet only took me nineteen years to feeger it out. End you are like, wot, twenty-five now?"

This teasing from his father always helped in the end. So Marc would again commit to trying to steer clear of his mother in order to avoid the feelings of inadequacy he would ultimately endure after speaking with her.

When it was finally time to leave Wisconsin, Marc's dad dropped him off at the airport in Milwaukee. After hugs, his dad handed him a couple hundred bucks and beamed with pride while he walked Marc to security. He was finally off.

A few hours later, the plane landed in San Diego, and Marc's cousin Lana was there waiting for him. The airline had lost one of Marc's bags, so they had plenty of time to soak up the San Diego airport, which they did, certainly, without being inconspicuous. Lana was apparently on something—meth, Marc would soon come to learn. She was loud, laughing. She hugged Marc furiously, introducing him to everyone, saying he was her cousin and wasn't he cute and how awesome it was to have him there in San Diego with her.

Marc filled out the lost baggage information, hoping to again see some of the few remaining belongings he had left in his world, and then they were off to "home." The first air Marc felt from San Diego was warm and comforting. It was about 10 PM, and the palm trees reflected the spotlight beams from the airport parking lot.

Lana drove a red Pontiac Firebird.

On the way to their home for the night, Marc learned that since Lana had quit the job at the ad agency, she no longer had the home on the beach that she had told him about (the whole thing made Marc question his cousin's relationship with her boss—no pay, yet staying at his beach home…), and Lana now was sleeping on the floor of her new manager's apartment—she had found a part time job at Lasers Today, a gaming and action arena. Marc would be joining her there, on the floor. He was thrilled…

Marc had thought $900 was enough for a single guy with a couple bags to get settled in somewhere, find a job, and create a life. Add the $200 his dad gave him, and he was set for a while. But he soon learned that San Diego was not the Midwest, and apartments there were much more than the $235 he had been paying for his one bedroom apartment in La Crosse. A two-day search finally netted him his very own studio apartment in Hillcrest. Marc was able to convince the manager to give him a couple months to pay the security deposit in full.

Hillcrest is the major gay area of San Diego, and to Marc, it felt like he'd hit the jackpot. He'd never seen anything like it before. Gay couples holding hands and nobody caring, not even flinching or turning to look!

Recharged, Marc was ready for the next step— finding a job.

21.

Jack, Jackson, JT, Jackio,

I am experiencing major withdrawal from our correspondence, being that it's been at a long red traffic light during my seemingly endless era of relocation. However, I am finally safe and secure in my own little (tiny) studio apartment in Hillcrest San Diego. My cousin Lana wanted to live on the beach, which would have been fine if I hadn't have been spoiled by my two months of solitary living in La Crosse. I decided I'd be a lot more comfortable in Hillcrest too as it's the major gay area in San Diego. It's crazy here by the way. Two guys can hold hands walking down the street and not a soul turns to look (except for me right now since it's so crazy, in a good way).

I finally got everything unpacked—4 boxes from UPS arrived Wednesday, and I got the last 5 today. Boy, what a mess I had! Everything's unpacked and kind of put away now, and I'm drinking a beer, smoking a Camel Light, and listening to the Indigo Girls—and doing what I like most—writing a letter to you.

Thanks for the holiday card. It's seriously the best card I've gotten, ever, and I will pack-rat it away forever. I truly believe you were God-sent into my life. You're amazing man—and you're an amazing man. I so want to come to Tucson to visit, not that I need to get out of SD already, but some good time with my JT would be excellent.

Ok, only been here a short time, and I've already met a man named...take a guess... Nope...guess again... Zen. Yes, his name is Zen. Well that's his nickname—his real name's Phillip, but they call him Zen cuz of his relaxed, constant meditative state. He totally reminds me of my friend Andreas from La Crosse, except Zen has like Gorilla hair coming out of the top of his shirt, from his chest I'm suspecting. He's a totally cool guy, though. Zen-like. I've also met a guy named Cham, but my favorite is a guy named Johnny. Beautiful inside and out. From LA, he's been in San Diego about 4 months. He's almost exactly like me, but he's had a rougher life so far and he's got a boyfriend. Damn! Oh well. The energy of God guides all I do and all that happens to me; however, I must say, "Hello God—I'm waiting..."

I've got 30 pages left to read in *Ismael*, by Daniel Quinn. Quite an interesting discussion inside those covers. Have you read it? I'm still planning on reading some of the books you've recommended, but I've got no budget for anything but food, beer, and cigarettes right now. I spent every last dime I came down (out) here with on this tiny (humble) studio.

January 3 on my little Zen calendar reads: "Those who consider external things important are stupid." Ha! Perfect! I think I must be stupid sometimes though. I just realized that that line relates, somewhat, to *Ismael*. Sorry, I seem to be babbling about nothing. I'm tired, and my creative spark has been gone for a couple weeks.

It has taken me a while to pull myself out of the muck I found myself in after graduation. My ma came up. I was seriously hoping we'd get along, and we did for awhile. But then she started in. I tried to show her that *Prayers of the Cosmos* book, but she ended up slamming it to the ground and saying that she didn't need to read any of these books written by men and that the only book she needed was the Bible. She says I need to be aware of these false prophets leading me down the wrong path, and I "need to be very careful." Ugh. I think I'll hang this up for now—getting frustrated again…

Ok, I'm back. It's like a week later. I called Chris in La Crosse, and he gave me your new address so I can send this off to you with MY new address.

Guess what I'm doing for employment now. Politics, man. Yuck, but it's fun and decent money for right now. I'm a petitioner—40 cents per signature—and I get to be outside all day making a fool of myself and talking to people. So far, it's a total blast! How's your job treating you? Good I hope!

So God brings a man into my life (there SO needs to be a new name/word for God—the Oversoul? The Source? the Universe??). He's my neighbor, totally a cool guy. A vegetarian, smart, totally into the Hindu religion. Interesting, cute, bald (shaven), but???

How's your love life? My cousin Lana and I have the same taste in men—we get in a lot of cat fights. Did I mention she's living here with me now? She begged and pleaded. It's tight (really tight), but she's family and I'm weak—soft. We'll see how it goes.

I can't wait to hear from you.
Talk to you soon Jackson!
-M

22.
Mr. Ortega:

Well, Mr. Sunny California, I'm gonna get all the guys now, stud boy, beach combin', head shavin', fresh outta college, thinks he's Mr. Big-Shot. How the hell are ya? No less than grand, I hope. Glad to hear you're settling in. Congratulations on the new-found employment. I hope you like it.

I've been wanting to tell you, on New Year's Eve, I went out with 4 or 5 other people my age and ended up, of all places, shakin' tail at some gay bar down on 4th Ave. It was a real blast (lots of quite buff-looking young men, in case you're wondering). I definitely had a real great time. I thought of you.

Well we pretty much got all our stuff moved into our new apartment. I definitely would like to find some place in between here and there to spend the night or two drunk and soaking in the scents and sounds of the crisp desert night and the bright star light. Sound good?

My friend Sarah should be flying in to Phoenix on the 8th to visit. I look forward to having another friend around since this certain other friend of mine—who shall remain nameless—we'll call him….Marc, got all finicky about "money" and "car insurance" and petty shit like that, and thus decided to opt for flying OVER AZ instead of driving through it. Anyway. Sarah is fun.

I have been playing guitar quite a bit lately. I enjoy it. I have recently met some people who also play guitars and pound on drums. Cool, very cool. They seem to be into the same R&B stuff (Rockabilly & Blues) I'm into. It should be fun. Lots of fun. The only negative thing would be, believe it or not, they probably like to smoke the dreamy greenie too much before playing. That's fine by me, but I've come to the conclusion that the wooga-wooga (weed) screws up my sense perceptions too much so I tend to sing like shit if I'm grabbing at dangling hay all night (way too high, I mean). We'll see how it goes. Ahhh, the life of a rock star, I tell ya…

[…still no understanding but a much wider base to stand ignorant on.

"Who am I?" asks country boy. White liberal middle class gen-X male pseudo intellectual reader of poetry-prose. Graphing the wares of indignation while my own voice tries to ring true to itself and those around me who find in a conversation mutually beneficial enlightenment. Time spent being friends or lovers and both.

Playing someone else's blues with minimal creative burst yet all in an individualized style. Reading about the African-American in an attempt to find some greater understanding in the dilemma of the veil of race consciousness. Oppressed and screwed over, free but second class first rate citizens are some.

World view? From Where? No depth, no width, no experience, no dice. Growing up white as white gets me eighteen years in a prison of privileged ignorance. Progressive steps come only if I search out the path.

The guns are somewhat loaded.]

So anyway... just a little rant...

Haiku #27...

Perched in rocks above
Mountain pass. Wind blows softly
Chasing the hawk's tail.

Haiku #15...

Moon lighting my smoke
As I drag Arizona
Highways...cool breezes.

Guess what (random though ALERT) I haven't changed that spare tire off my car yet, and I've been to Flagstaff and back on it. Damn lucky so far...

Anyway my soul brother, I hope everything is going no less than great for you out there in Cali.

Take care.

O, by the way, I'm back on meat. Just poultry, but o-well.

Be safe.

Jackson

23.

Howdy Jackson!

I arrived home from work this evening to find a pleasant surprise in the mailbox—a cool letter from my JT. It's good to hear you're having fun and getting to know some people. It would be awesome to meet you somewhere in the middle of the desert to talk shit and drink plenty of beers.

By the way, butthead, I didn't see you looking into the sky and waving as I flew by/over Arizona. And thanks for not trying to show me your Yin/Yang as we passed by—your white ass may have blinded the pilot. Ha!

It is very difficult for me to write poetry right now. I need alone time and don't get much of it living with my cousin in this small studio apartment. That's okay for a while though, I guess. Last Friday, Lana and I went to a hardcore punk rock band called Shout Out Hoods who played at Bodie's downtown. Tell you what, I like the stuff a little better live, but my ears were ringing for about 2 and a half days after. I woke up Saturday morning wondering why I couldn't hear very well. Needless to say I finally figured it out. Duh!

Did I tell you about our mist storm we had here last week? It was seriously just misting out for about three hours—many accidents, power outages—including many traffic lights. It seems that people freak out here when the sun's not shining, which, might I add, is very rare.

My neighbor friend downstairs—the cute one with the question mark in my mind—gets the Hare Krishna *Back to Godhead* magazine. Lana and I just had a conversation about that neighbor's voice. She says he talks "kind of flamy," but I prefer to call it "speech like a gentle pastel-colored rose—hypnotic to all senses" and "very sexy." Anyhow, he just bummed me one of his magazines—quite interesting stuff, very transcendental, although some of the ideas are contradictory to themselves—sort of like the Bible, I guess. I suggest checking your local library and browsing through a recent edition.

I liked your desert solitude rant. I wish there were some peaceful desert settings nearby here that I could retreat to. What does "the guns are somewhat loaded" refer to? Do I need to be worried?

Today I was on the busy corner outside my house, collecting signatures, and a woman who was on the corner collecting spare change started bitching at me cuz I was on her corner.

"Get your own damn corner," she said. I wasn't, didn't even want to collect money, obviously. In fact I was getting people to stop right in front of her so she could yell at them—yes, she was kind of a rude panhandler. I'm afraid tomorrow she's gonna bring a knife and scare me off her corner. Anger breeds anger, you know. Perhaps she was channeling my mother...

Well, JT-bro, I am now ready to hit the flour pot. So I'll rapper up and popper in the box tomorrow. Hey, take care of your awesome self. Stay inspired. Chatatcha soon man.

Nature-is-god-is-love,
Marc.

24.
Hey Doug,

Sounds like you're in a pretty hip little community/neighborhood there. I'm at work right now, still on the night shift. O-well. *Strange Brew— The Adventures of Bob and Doug McKenzie* is on TBS now. Classic flick! I love it.

I think you're getting a little crazy with how amazing you think I am. I am about two bricks shy of the amazement you've built with your life. I think we should find a place somewhere between SD and AZ with a campground and pitch a tent for 2-3 nights. A few cases of beer, maybe a few dozen pens & some paper and plenty of good company. I am really itching to get out of town. If I were gay, I bet we could be a fun couple, huh? Too presumptuous? Then again, maybe the fact that I'm not is why we "click" as well as we do.

This movie is a beauty, any hosehead worth a stick of butter knows the value of this classic comedy. My friend Sarah is leaving soon, on Saturday (she's been visiting for the last week). After that I want to get out of town and camp. I don't care how cold it gets—I wanna spend the night by the camp fire, drinking beer, smoking whatever, drinking Canadian whiskey straight out of the bottle—just relaxing, hopefully with a good friend, a male friend anyway. It's weird, as much as I longed for some female companionship before Sarah got here, I somehow will feel relieved when she goes.

I'm reading a very interesting book. *Outlaw Culture: Resisting Representations,* by bell hooks. She's a cultural critic, black feminist who critiques our society from one end to the other. I dig it. I'm faithful to the idea that if the "white folks" of our nation/culture want to really know what's wrong, they need to use the voice of the oppressed Americans as a mirror to themselves. hooks talks of the white, patriarchal colonial imperialists who perpetuate the status quo by supporting feminists who only really speak in support of the system as it is and don't really offer radical or revolutionary ideas. I dig her spirit and the take she has on our society. I think you would like it as well.

I get worried sometimes that too easily the privilege of my skin color and the structure of our society, as far as serving the white-male imperialistic status quo, goes unnoticed and used, abused, by myself and others who consider themselves forward-thinking people. How can we get away from it? Can we? Where does change start?

I'm now watching *Kung Fu*, the old TV series.

The last thing I want to do is be a hypocrite, but am I innately bound to failure because of my upbringing and skin color/ethnicity. Can we get away from serving the status quo to a place that recognizes progressive radical/revolutionary thought serving people regardless of class, gender, or race? Sometimes, often, I think it CANNOT happen. It's all so deeply engrained in our American cultural experience. Where's the simplicity in these issues? There is none! Where's the truth? It's too much! I think I'll overheat if I keep on this rampage of thought and self-scrutiny.

I like these old Kung Fu programs. I dig the Eastern wisdom, of course.

Well that was last night. Tonight I'm contemplating my happiness, wondering where it is. I thought when I left La Crosse, my happiness would surface as my blues dissolved. Why!? Why has my happiness gone? It isn't that I'm all depressed. I guess I'm more upset or angry, but I really don't know why. Really. How do people maintain a greater degree of happiness, satisfaction with their lives? What the fuck am I missing? I have a feeling the solution may be one of something simple (of course figuring it out is the difficult part—and I have to remind myself it's the fun part as well— supposed to be at least). I am confused. Any suggestions? Maybe you could engage your friend Zen in my dilemma, see if there is any worthy advice there.

The guns are somewhat loaded... Don't worry, just a figurative phrase meant to represent my psychological state of being somewhat ready to "unload" the mental ammunition that's been building in my melon. Just my way of saying "get ready" I'm about to explode/unload/fire. I don't feel that way all the time, but I sure as hell do some of the time. But then that's just ego wanting to be unleashed.

Speaking of ego, I've been meaning to comment on your mother. First of all, I'm sorry you're having to deal with her bringing you down all the time. You do a good job staying positive though, for the most part. Keep your head up. One thing I ponder often is what the conservative Christians think about why God gave humans brains. If we were only meant to obey and read one book, then what a waste of the awesome invention of the brain, and what an enormous waste of our creativity!

So, you've met some cool cats as well. Glad to hear it. I'd like to come visit some time. Do you have any ideas about how long you plan to stay in SD? I think I might be staying in Tucson into the summer months, at least until May 1.

Have you ever been to Virginia? I've been wondering lately what it would be like to live there. Dave, my old roommate in La Crosse, is moving to

Chicago, but I don't know if I really want to go there, although it would be excellent to live with Dave again. Have you picked up the new Live Indigo Girls Disc yet? It is good. Real good.

Well, hoser, I think I am going to wrap this up and get it out to you. Take care and let me know if you can/want to do that desert rendezvous. I am looking forward to getting out of town for a night (preferably two).

Peace Bro.
Bob.

JT got out for a couple days. Marc had since quit his job peddling signatures for CalSurge and was waiting to hear about his application at the Veggie Deli across the street from his apartment. There wasn't much cash to speak of so Jack made the solo trek out to San Diego to visit.

Jack was pleased to finally meet Lana and Ted. They all let loose then, drinking beers most of the night. JT brought his guitar for some rock n' blues 'n billy strummin'. Marc joined in as usual, making drums out of kitchen pots, and Lana and Ted followed suit, Lana with a set of spoons, a skill she'd learned from her mother, and Ted crumpling up the morning's want-ads.

After the jam, they all decided to go out. It was late, after midnight, but the gay bars were busy as usual on a Saturday night.

Jack was impressed with Lana's skill on the pool table. Lana and Marc had spent several evenings together at the bars. Lana had all along refused to pay rent, put it off actually, explaining to Marc that she'd have some rent money after the next paycheck, but then explaining that she had to get this or that fixed on her car or she had to pay for a recent doctor visit. Something always came up. But Lana didn't have any qualms with paying for Marc to go out to the bars with her, and so he did.

At the bars in San Diego, if you wanted a chance to play pool, you'd have to put your name on the list on a chalkboard and then wait your turn. Winners kept playing and had the choice of whether they wanted to play singles or doubles.

Having played quite a bit of pool in his dad's basement as well as at the bars in La Crosse, Marc was a decent pool shot himself, but if the table was playing singles when Lana or Marc's name came up, it would always be Lana who won the table for them. And she *always* won the table, beating out some of the best pool players in the city.

She was such a solid shot! The best part was her lack of hesitation; she never had to line up a shot. She'd strut around the table, bend over, and immediately take her next shot, no studying, no aiming, nothing. Inevitably, her opponents would be lost in disbelief, their heads shaking like drunken bobble-head dolls.

When Lana sank the eight ball, she'd finish the game off with a quick blow at the tip of her pool cue, a confident, albeit cocky, finish. Marc absolutely loved this. As a result, he enjoyed her company and kept her around. Jack and Ted sat at a tall bar table nearby and rolled their eyes in awe at Lana's nonchalant skill.

The next morning Jack and Marc had a chance to check out some of the local Hillcrest book and music stores, get a Tribeans coffee, and talk about some of the more important stuff like the nature of God, man, energy, and light. In no time, Jack was back on the road on his way home to Tucson. They both thought it was too short of a visit.

25.
Dear Oprah,

Thanks for taking the journey to rainy San Diego. I had a fantastic time and hope you did also. It was great to see you after so many months. Lana and Ted are fighting over you. They both think you're "darling." Ain't that cute! Ted was inspired by your butt cheek and is already out today getting a yin/yang on his forearm. Since you've been gone, I've written about 4 pages of creative dribble each day. Perhaps your visit inspired the creativity to again seep through my fingertips.

Today, Lana and I were at a second-hand clothing store. Lana was trying on some beautiful poke-a-dot dresses and stuff. Lots of fun.

Anyhow, just wanted to get you a quick note to say thanks for visiting. I'm going to get back to writing while I'm still hungry for it.

Peace, Sis.
Uma.

26.
Marc,

Well, I made it back, no problems. I had such a good time when I was visiting. Even though I was only there for a day, essentially, it felt quite good. I'm not sure how to express the way I feel, because that is mostly why I say I had such a good time. It <u>felt</u>

good. Maybe it was the vibe (the nice, friendly, happy vibe) of Hillcrest or maybe it was just the fact that I was out, on the road, on my own, on a little bit of an adventure.

The feeling I have is almost like something inside of me, a contentment or satisfaction type of thing, within the depths of my psyche, has been renewed or recharged, maybe even discovered. The nice people I met and the little walks and good conversation. It was ALL good. Believe me, I enjoyed it more than you'll know. It makes me, seriously, consider the possible reality of moving/living/working in sunny southern Cali... Seriously.

It was good to see you again, to see the changes you've made, to be able to talk to a familiar friend again. I very much appreciate the time you took out (even though you're unemployed—bum—and broke), and I appreciate your concern for my being there. How much of a reality check is it for me to think about moving to S.D.? Just musing on the possibilities, but it would be, as far as I can tell, a progressive step forward.

It's like this: I've been trying to keep in check all the options I have in front of me as far as what I could do and where I could go in May, after my lease is up. I've been talking to a couple people I've met here about moving east (Buffalo, NY)...but...for some reason, it just doesn't sound, or _feel_, like the "right thing," like it wouldn't be a progressive step forward. The guys are nice enough and we'd be set up in an old Victorian style house in West Buffalo, which would be ok, but (again that big <u>but</u>) it just seems as though it might be a regressive move for me.

On the other hand, I could go to Flagstaff. That would be cool—mountains, hippies, cool stuff, smaller town, but I'm not sure Flag. has anything more to offer me than Tucson. I suppose I could go to Chicago with Dave, but I don't think so—I've done the Midwest.

So what about Diego? Well, I met some cool people, I'd have at least one good friend who I trust already there, it's on the Pacific, I've never lived in Cali... I don't know, if I could say that I feel I could retain these positive emotional and physical feelings that I have gained through my visit throughout an extended stay in SD, I would be sure about a move there.

I don't know Marco, what do you think? I've got a little time to decide, what would you say about the possibility of being roommates? (Now let's take stock here. I am just wondering to you about some of these things, obviously, nothing solid is being discussed at this time. Also I wouldn't want to assume too much about you even wanting to share an apt. or any other such thing... so, be aware, I'm aware that this is all theory knowhatimean?)

So anyway, this is somewhat of a thank-you-for-your-hospitality note and also somewhat of a what-am-I-going-to-do-with-my-life note, as you've read.

I hope (but do not expect) that something, a sign of some sort, will give me insight-guidance-direction about where I could go that would help me progress in life (not stay where I am, not regress) to "the next (or another) level," whatever the hell that is. Wherever the hell that is. I don't know. And also, when I ask "what do you think," I guess I'm asking more about what you feel. Obviously I'm not looking for you to answer my questions or solve my dilemma, just asking your opinion.

I will find an answer, or it will find me. One way or the other, I will be able to see my way along this long, dark path, this trail of unanswered questions and too questioned answers...

So anyway, thanks again for everything. Let me know how you are. I want to say I miss ya, but that would be all sappy and shit, so, I guess, I look forward to seeing you again. Take care of yourself, and good luck in the job search.

(Webster's definition of koan: n. a riddle in the form of a paradox used in Zen Buddhism as an aid to meditation and a means of gaining intuitive knowledge or spiritual awakening.)

Until next time,
J

P.S. I remember specifically the look on your face as I pulled away, before I waved, it didn't seem good. Is everything ok? Just wondering.

27.
Dear Jackson,

What I think does not matter. It never has. I am a dumb jerk and nobody likes me. Nobody wants me to work for them either. They won't even pay me $4.25 an hour cuz I guess I'm over-qualified to flip veggie-burgers. However, I am under-qualified and haven't enough experience to edit the work of a journalist before publishing. I'm a slow reader anyhow. What I think I'm saying is that I'm shocked and hurt that you would even dare to mock me by asking for my input in your life. I think it's rude and totally unacceptable because I am a nothing, and my life means the same—nothing.

You can do anything your little heart desires in May. But if you're going to push me into telling you what I think, I guess I'll have to tell you this: The only thing—aesthetic-wise—missing from San Diego is nature. There does not seem to be enough of it. I enjoy trees, rocks (mountains), and vast spaces (I need to be able to breathe), and there's not much of it here (at least not much I can access without a car or money). However, the social atmosphere (for the most-part) is so calming, soothing, loving, and hang-outy that I do love this place regardless of the lack of the natural setting.

Sorry about my piss-poor attitude. I just got off the phone with the mother figure. She started in again but then said that she wasn't judging me and I shouldn't judge her for just telling me what the Bible says. She says she wants to make sure the Lord hears her tell me that she will never recognize (or accept, obviously) my "so-called lifestyle" because it is wrong, according to the Bible. She said that the fact that Christ came and died on the cross does not negate the Old Testament, just adds to it. She said that God is "just" and that even though He loves us, He won't allow sin into Heaven. I'm just stewing right now. Break time...

Okay I'm back. It's been a few days so I had to reread what I'd written, and I've got to say I almost ripped it up. But since you're my JT, I know you'll just take it for what it's worth. Yin/Yang, right? Your butt-cheek speaks to me (you should see Ted's arm—way cool, sort of hidden on the back, underside of his forearm).

I think you would enjoy living out here. I wouldn't even mind perhaps moving to Pacific Beach in May. Maybe I'd have a beater-car by then—who knows. I love Hillcrest, but it's hard to meet guy-friends cuz everyone (including myself) thinks that if you want to do something with another guy, then you're hitting on him. So it's difficult to get to know someone without wondering if they're trying to have sex with you. I do not like that part of Hillcrest. PB wouldn't be like that.

A huge suggestion: If you are serious about doing this, start looking for a job now. The job market here sucks, although you may be more marketable than I am.

Sometimes I miss the Midwest, but that's probably expected. A lot of the time, lately, I want to go into a corner and cry for days. A lot of the time I want to take a short survival course and then move into the mountains and live off the land for seven years after filing bankruptcy. I think the only thing I'm qualified to do (at least, possibly, a little qualified) is write, but one needs money to exist on in order to find the time needed to write anything worthwhile.

Have I told you that I want to go into a corner and cry? Cuz my clothes were stolen, cuz my bike was stolen, cuz I have no money and no job, cuz (and I am being selfish here) my dad goes on a Caribbean cruise instead of making sure his flesh and blood has a roof over his head (maybe the roof should be on my head, like the wicked witch of the West (Midwest)). I'm getting really good at whining and begging.

By the way, I'm glad you're so happy!

I'm going to become a hermit. The UPS guy finally came and took my computer monitor (they busted it while shipping it out here)—I hope I can at least trust him. I feel as though I should just raise my arms to the moon and scream out, "Come and get it. Take all I have. Strip me of myself. In fact, you might as well take my entire soul too." This fucking world pisses me off.

Wow, I thought I was feeling better, but look at this negativity just swoop right back in… It's like it becomes dominant, addictive. It's like all the cells in my body are fighting to be fed, craving the poor me drug. If I recognize this will it wane? Will it even out? I am hopeful, but then someone comes and steals something from me, whether it's clothing, my pride, my self-respect, my everlasting life…

You know, if everything in this life (all our experiences, that is) is meant to teach us what we need to know before we live for eternity in our spiritual form—(which I used to think of as Heaven)—why in the world do we need to learn to not trust people! Doesn't trust follow from love? Isn't eternity with God in "Heaven" based fully on love and goodness—isn't trust inherent? Will we need to be aware of who we can and cannot trust in Heaven? Am I starting to believe again that there is a Heaven with pearly-white gates and the Big Man seated in a giant throne? Is my mother still having an effect on me?

No, no, no! I can't let it happen! The conclusion I MUST accept is that Heaven—as we've been raised to understand it—DOES NOT EXIST. Physical death must send our spirits into a plane where not only good spiritual energies flow, but also evil, semi-evil, or just buzz energy exists. Perhaps we have to learn to watch out for which spirits we can trust in that realm…

Ok, Ted's here now, and I can't concentrate anymore. I'll talk more to you about this soon.

Peace and Cheerios,
Marc.

I feel the need to catch you up on some of the events that were going on in San Diego in between the letters, some of the things Jack learned during his visit. Obviously, Marc was pretty much in the dumps at the time of this most recent letter. You see, although he enjoyed her company at the bars, the whole roommate situation with his cousin Lana was beginning to wear on Marc.

The guys Lana brought home did not please Marc whatsoever. There was the straight drag queen, whose autobiographical book that he had entrusted to Lana for her to read she would not return because she had ended up fearing him, thinking he was out to get her, a common paranoia among meth addicts and schizophrenics. Then there was Rusty, the one she would have sex with in the closet of their studio apartment and who "borrowed" Marc's bike one morning to "run and turn a job application in real quick" and then never returned, ever—nor would Marc's new Gary Fisher. Lana heard Rusty had gone to jail on drug charges, and she at least spent the time to track him down and mail him a letter asking where the bike was, which Marc thought was nice. But apparently Rusty had used it to pay for some of his drug bills and no longer knew where the bike might be.

Then, of course, Marc's clothes where stolen from the laundry room of his apartment building. Not once, but twice. And Lana's attitude was changing, getting worse. Marc had to talk to her. He knew it was the drugs she was using that were changing her more and more—she was spending more time in the bathroom, picking at her face. But she always denied it. He had heart-to-hearts with her. He tried yelling at her. He brought home literature on the effects of meth-use. But nothing opened her eyes to her denial.

Marc seemed swarmed with negativity, and it didn't seem like it could get much worse. To Marc, San Diego was winning. He did however have one small thread of hope left; he still had Ted, a nice young man he desperately wanted to get to know better.

28.
2/10/96.

"I want to go to the mountains," he cried. "I need to go. But how am I going to get there?"

I cried. I cried because I wanted to go too. I needed to go, but my mind would not allow me to let go of the bullshit responsibilities in the populated world. I guess it was the fear. Afraid that financial responsibilities would not be met. Afraid that friends would not respect me. Afraid that people would say I gave up. Afraid that I would believe I gave up. Afraid of my own guilt.

But still I want to go.

There is no attitude in the mountains, very little pollution, no infestation. Why have I thought about this move for so long, only to awaken to family attitudes, disgust, and a friend who has dreamed that he must get to the mountains, a friend who did not know of my dreams to go? Should I make a decision now?

No. I must wait until my driving questions are answered. Then, if everything points to the mountains, I will go.

JT, just a thought—provoked by Lana's attitude lately and the fact that Ted and I just had to get rid of scabies last night. If you start itching, it may be that.

Sorry.
Marc.

29.
Marc,

I could hit walls, scream, kick my way into tear dropping depths of frustration and angst. My life is stale, rotting in a can of worms called these here United States. I am American; I have no sense of what that means. How could I? I need the objectivity, the subjectivity, the experience of being out, away, alone, the stranger in some other strange land. When? How? I don't know. Maybe never. Maybe some day when it is too late already.

Every so often, I'm okay with being confined to these self-imposed trappings of loans, education, and ignorance. Most of the time, though, I want to be somewhere else, speaking a different language, absorbing, analyzing a different cultural milieu. You've probably heard me bitch about this so many times before that you, along with the rest of my friends, are getting sick of it. Well, well, what can I say?

I keep seeing these employment opportunities to teach conversational English in Korea. Is that the answer? Where will it get me? What will I have more of when I return? Depth? Knowledge of self and others to a greater extent? A completely different perspective on life? I don't know.

I sent a cover letter and résumé to a summer camp in Jackson WY the other day, and I am using the facilities at the U of A Career Services office to scan nationwide job opportunities. I am hoping something will come through and make me happy one of these days.

So anyway, I suppose you get the impression that I'm all pissed about life and shit. Not really, just frustrated. I'm actually in a fairly good mood. Perhaps your negativity has been a bit contagious. No blame though, my man. I choose my own emotions, always. Of course I'm at work and not liking it very much.

If you haven't read *Siddhartha* by Hermann Hesse yet, I recommend it. I imagine Ted has read it. I am re-reading it and gain insight from every page.

Lately I have been wishing I were in a relationship, a mellow, rewarding one—although in ways I am glad I'm not; it would only make it harder to move on out of Tucson. Although sometimes I want a little human touch, closeness, you know, not necessarily sex but something. Although if one gets a little, more is always getting closer, more desirable. I have to say that I am not at this time filled with a lot of optimism for my (personal) immediate future or the future of our society as a whole. I'm gonna put this aside and hope to be feeling better when I pick it up again...

Well, I guess I'm feeling a bit better. This week has been frustrating in that, until today, the Career Services office had nothing new to offer me. Even today the new choices don't really excite me to the point that I'm all hot and sweaty.

Do you have a job yet? Bud, I hope so. Pretty soon you'll be sleeping on the street or something. I wish you luck if you still need it.

I haven't been writing shit lately. No inspiration I guess. I really don't have much else of newsworthy info to shout out about. I guess maybe I'll just send this much out to let you know I haven't forgotten about your bald ass over there in sunny CA.

Take care.
Write back—please!
Jackson.

This is the shot that Jack took of Marc as he descended from the mountain trail to their campsite just outside of Santa Fe. Marc says he had just finished meditating.

Apache-Sitgreaves National Forest, Arizona. This shot was taken by Marc as Jack drove down the Mogollon Rim, into the clouds, and through the elk.

Jack in Box Canyon.

This is Marc in Patagonia, Arizona, making his attempt,
although futile, at cracking open a geode.

30.

Jackson,

Great to hear from you. You did not sound too happy on the phone or in your letter. However, at least you spent some time to write some things out—that always seems to help me. At least you still have your sense of humor too. Don't ever hesitate to vent—I'm not going to (hesitate). If I fed you some of my negativity, I apologize, and I will try to balance that out with a bit of positive news.

So I guess raising my arms to the "Heavens" and giving up all control over my life to the energy force of the universe has helped me to finally change all the bad luck I've been experiencing in the cold city of San Diego. Smiles.

I had a bit of a freak out last week. I kind of started dating a guy named Todd—he looks/walks almost exactly like alien Joe. Anyhow, he told me last Monday that he has HIV. It didn't really freak me out, because we never did anything that would have given it to me, at least that I remembered...

Tell you the truth, I've been living the last 4 years of my life too worried about being tested—I've basically assumed I've had it. What I was really stressing out about though was realizing that getting tested was only the first step. Then I would have to decide whether or not I should keep seeing Todd. The thing is, I wanted to keep seeing him, but obviously I didn't want to be positive—crazy mixed emotions.

So, Lana and I went through crying spells for two days—Tuesday when I told her (because I told her I thought I might be positive) and then Wednesday before I went in to get tested. I'm too much of a freakoid to do the free test and then wait two weeks to get the results so I paid $15 for the 24 hour results. I asked the guy that took my blood whether I could bring support the next day when I came to get my results. He said that if I get results the next day, then I wouldn't need support, so I immediately knew that the phone call the next day to find out if my results were in would give me my answer.

It took the guy 3 or 4 minutes to find out if my results were in or not, during which time I was shaking like mad, biting my fingernails, tearing up (crying), and smoking all at the same time. They really should figure out a better system. Remember, up above, when I said I'd been living my life basically assuming I have it? Well, I'm leaving a little bit of truth out. I actually <u>thought</u> I had it. I used to get these scaly sores on the sides of my hips which freaked me out, and I know at least one guy I've been with is now dying. But I've been too scared to get tested.

Anyhow, the results were in. I went in and, yes— they were negative (non-reactive) at this time. Woo-Woo. (I guess the scaly sores were just dry skin or something.)

But then there was my dilemma: should I continue seeing Todd? I decided I would—and just live safely...

But then I found out he was still doing crystal meth. I'd specifically told him how I felt about that, and he knew that if he kept doing it I'd be gone. Lana knew how I felt too, obviously, but who, of all people, do I catch Todd doing it with? You guessed it—Lana! Fucking bitch sometimes!

So, Todd still wants to quit, but I'm not going to be anything more than support for him. Besides, if he keeps doing crystal with having HIV, he'll probably be dead in only a few months.

It's funny, the guy that helped me catch them smoking is in town for the weekend from Phoenix, supposedly visiting Lana—she fasted for 7 days in order to lose weight so she didn't look fat when Dave got here. Then she pushes him off on me for the entire weekend and doesn't want anything to do with him—probably because he caught her doing the heavy drugs and confronted her on it. I'm glad he did—I'll have a few words to say to her after he leaves this afternoon!! They'll be <u>choice</u> words, of course. Enough about that.

My dad told me to start keeping a journal about the interesting events I experience living with Lana, then perhaps sometime in the future I could write a lighthearted novel about it—like the straight cross-dresser she befriended then de-friended—or the freak Christopher, whom you met, the one that Lana likes to lead on to stroke her power trips, even though she'll never be his gf—or the other freak Rick (whom you also met) who sits outside our building for three hours waiting for us to come home so he

115

can come inside for hours uninvited and mooch everything we don't have. In the long run, these stories will be kind of funny, I imagine—maybe?

Yes, Ted has heard of Hermann Hesse's *Siddhartha* and has read it several times.

I'm also searching for the purpose of my life. Have I told you that I'm considering taking a survival course and then moving to the mountains? No telling what a person can accomplish with some peace and solitude—and boy-howdy do I need some.

May I scream? Thanks.

Anyhow, I have a little peace of mind now that I have a job (at a nearby Lux Queen down the hill from Hillcrest), so maybe some creativity will be able to begin flowing from my "melon" (as you say) soon.

It is extremely nice hearing from you.

Peace and an energetic pen.
Marc.

31.
Brother Ortega,

So good to hear from you, and in good spirits as well. Yes! I am <u>very</u> glad for you that you got yourself tested for HIV. I was in suspense as I read your letter, then finally breathed a sigh of relief when I got to the outcome.

I am at work, reading Jack London. Yes. I have been inspiring myself for what will hopefully be an outdoor summer. *To Build a Fire and Other Stories* is the collection I picked up for $2.25 used. I'm hooked. I've also been reading some Langston Hughes and James Baldwin. Good authors. Isn't Pat Buchanan the best out of all those hopeless candidates? I think so. The weather here is getting better. Last week it was all overcast and chilly. It has been warming up gradually this week. I was <u>totally joking</u> about Buchanan. I think he's a bigot piece of shit bastard. Anyway, I hope the weather gets better as these days and nights roll on by.

Have you been writing lately? Me, not much in the way of anything, besides some letters that get a little nutty.

Crystal meth, huh? My advice there would be to not get involved. That shit is bad news. Then again, you know that so I don't have to grill you on the dangers of hard drugs.

I've decided that I want to spend the summer around a lot of big trees. I don't want to go back out east. I think I might rather stay in Tucson. Well, maybe not. I don't know. I too, lately, have been seriously pondering the purpose of my existence. I haven't come up with anything substantial yet. Maybe you and I can find some neighboring mountains to live upon, maybe get together once every week or 10 days to see how things are going. Sound good? Alright it's a plan. Yeah, right.

I made a progressive step forward, truly, the other day. Out of nowhere. I was driving, fussing over mistakes that I've made in my life. All these mistakes just kept swirling in my mind, dragging me down—and then I realized (and this "organic" sort of realization has never really happened to me before) that: sure I've made mistakes, plenty of them—but—look at all the progress I've made with my life. I could have <u>easily</u> turned out to be a white-trash piece of shit. But I feel I have come a long way from those "roots" and developed myself into a forward thinking productive citizen.

I've done a lot for myself—and—will continue to do so through any progeny I may have. But for me, that is/was a great step. Years ago, I believe, I would have just drowned in the self-induced negativity I was producing. But, from within, came up an optimistic view. Genuinely a progressive step forward. Yay Jack! Of course that's not to say I'll never engage in pessimism again, but just having an optimistic thought beat the pessimism out of my head is definitely something that never happened—to that extent—before.

I miss Sarah, sometimes a little more than maybe I should. Sometimes I wonder if I should just stay in Tucson and be here when she moves here (a move she'd been planning for years regardless of me being here). But then I think I just need to do for me still, that I can't sit somewhere and wait for a woman, even if we get along well. If it is meant to be, it will be. That is what we have said to each other all along.

Well, only 50 minutes left of my shift, and I need to count meds and write the charts.

Take care and be true.
JT

32.
YEAHH, Marco!

My man, my mentor, my goodness, I wish you were in town. I know I wrote you last, and I am anxiously waiting to hear from you (as always), but hell, a letter's a letter is a letter. No?

I am currently on shift (overnight, still, of course). As far as work goes, well, same old shit—bull. I have been actively looking for other employment, nationwide, with little response as of yet. But I am waiting. Who knows where I am going (or why for that matter)—but I am going somewhere. How can I not?! Always progressing, even if I'm standing still. Evolution surrounds.

I went to the park again yesterday—have I told you of my newfound pastime? Instead of lying in bed trying to sleep all day, I've been going to a park on the U of A campus and sleeping under the sway of palm trees and AZ breezes. <u>Damn</u> nice. So anyway, I went to the park yesterday and played my guitar for a while until I broke a string, lied in the sun, read some Jack London, kicked my hack around and just plain hung out for a few hours. It was a beautiful day, as was today, when I did the same thing (minus the guitar).

I'm feeling fairly okay these days although I do feel the anxiety bubble up occasionally, sometimes unnervingly, but I get through. I will feel 3000 times better when I have something lined up for the summer. Sure I can always stay here—and get either better hours or a different job—but I'd rather move on down that road—Ahh, The Road.

Well, my non-dating spell is up. Yessirree, I gots me a date! I was watching a band play (Greasy Chicken) at a bar, Jaime's, and all of a sudden there was a young woman on the stool next to me. Somehow we got to talking (me being nicely loaded helped, I'm sure), and it turned out that she's been in Tucson about as long as I have. She came here to get away from, seemingly, a bad relationship (if memory serves), AND she went to college with a major in— sit down—Psychology. Yes, I <u>know</u> I swore off psych. majors, but she (Stephanie) was very personable and gave me good eye contact. So we're going to go out on Sunday. It should be fun; at least I'll be sober. I just hope I don't make a fool out of myself, but really, I think it'll go just fine. Definitely "no expectations"—how could there be? Just gonna cruise on with what feels right. Damn Right!

So anyway, if you want a good read in the realm of psych, pick up *Man and His Symbols* and read Part 3, "The Process of Individuation" by M.L. von Franz (a Jungian). I just finished it—it has some very

"Celestine" commentaries. Reinforces my ideas about going my own way, listening to "the voice" within and "following my bliss" (per Joseph Campbell). Sometimes I really wonder how much sense any of what I say makes.

So, my main amigo. I hope everything is going well. Take care of yourself.

Paz y felicidad.
Olé!
Jack

33.
Yo JT,

I found two jobs. I think I told you about the Lux Queen and now at Tribeans so I've been working a lot and am tired a lot. Since getting through training and starting at Tribeans (yes, the one across the street), I've been able to put my two weeks in at the Lux Queen job, which I hated (Luxury in San Diego was not nearly the same as in La Crosse, and I was having transportation issues anyways).

We've recently had two house-guests from the Midwest—one of Lana's friends and one of mine. Plus my cousin's boyfriend-at-the-time was living here against my wishes. Lana asks me, "What do you think of Ryan living here?" Needless to say, I started laughing until I figured out she was serious—huh? What the fuck was she thinking? Where the fuck is her mind? AhhHaa! It is lost in the white dust of the clear bowl she calls "living."

Anyhow, luck came this last weekend. Our landlord told Ted of a two bedroom she has available in the next building over. He knows everything I have to deal with living with Lana so he asked me if I wanted to share the apartment. I guess I don't have to say that I'm moving out April 1. I'm not exactly sure what Lana's going to do, but that's not for me to deal with. She's the one who's had a job all this time, but I seem to be able to pay more rent than she ever can. I guess all her cash is going to her little drug problem, as usual. This weekend, she totally broke out with acne all over her body—her face was all puffy, and she was crying for hours. She blamed it on the soap, but Ted called her on it being a reaction some people get when they come off of a drug binge, and she got all defensive on Ted and started crying again. I'm sure that's what it was. Things keep on moving—one small but interesting event at a time.

I went surfing yesterday. I actually got to the point where I was able to stand up on the board. For the brief moment I was up, I felt freer than I have since skiing at Steamboat. It's almost like the wave was my mountain. This guy I met in a Tribeans training class lives in PB and has 5 boards and 5 wet suits in his living room. He's letting me borrow and acting as my surf coach for the meantime. I'm still considering moving to the mountains though. We'll see how it goes being Ted's roommate.

My love/dating life completely and utterly sucks right now—the only cute and interesting person I've met in a long time is that surfer-boy, but he's straight. Oh, I'm in a rut. We went to Tijuana last Friday, got all fucked up and passed out on the trolley home—good thing my friend Sue was along to wake us up.

JT, Jackson, I need some nature!

I just HAD ANOTHER LOAD OF FUCKING CLOTHES STOLEN—FUCKING JACK OFF FUCKERS IN THIS FUCKING STATE! I CAN'T FUCKING WRITE RIGHT NOW—

Ok, so I've calmed down a little bit. It's a few days later. My aunt and uncle were in town for the weekend. It was nice seeing some family besides Lana—I kinda needed someone to talk to about it (her).

So, where did we leave off? Oh, my clothes—they're gone—oh well—I've still got my health—and in a hundred years we'll all be dead anyhow, right? On Friday I actually <u>turned</u> on the surfboard. Talk about some aching muscles—that's some tough work, man!

Depending on how cheap I can find a plane ticket, I'm considering purchasing one to Tucson soon. Oh, pondering a little vacation is bringing tingles to my neck hairs.

I've been trying to figure out why I've been so blah blah lately, and I've come to two conclusions: 1) a lack of nature, and 2) a misalignment in my spiritual path. I think it began with Ted constantly talking about Krishna and his (Ted's) Hindu beliefs. Initially he sounded like he knew what he was talking about, and most of what he said I could understand. Then came the contradictions. Now I often have quite an enjoyable time making Ted think about some of the things he says. We usually have fun bickering back and forth. But now my beliefs, which acted as the foundation for my happiness and creativity, have been disturbed.

I've decided not even to buy any new clothes anymore if they're just going to get stolen. Perhaps a little basic foundation will set me back on my own path again. I love Ted and all, but I hope he doesn't drive me nuts living with him. He's constantly talking about his sex-capades too, which bothers me for three reasons: 1) I really don't care, 2) it sort of makes me jealous, and 3) I wouldn't want him telling his other friends about our personal bed-acts—not that they're too frequent or anything.

I broke down yesterday and bought a John Denver CD, and now I can't stop listening to it. I wish all it took was sunshine on my shoulders to make me happy—damn it! I am creatively flatlined, and the lack of sleep is contributing to the sloppiness of my writing. I'll call the travel agencies tomorrow.

Miss you JT.
Marc.

34.

Marckie!

Hey, hey, hey, what's the word? Ahh, my mind is running on a low tank of (energy) fuel here and now 3 AM on shift useless as ever and anxious to be done with these bullshit hours of relative indentured servitude. Whatever... I'm sick of these hours (still). I know it's the same bitch I've had for the past 3 months, but it is as true as ever.

But, there is light at the end of this particular tunnel, and I can see it growing stronger just about every day. The light is of the northern variety, of the Wisconsin breed. Yes, I have found a summer job back up north and will be leaving this desert kiln of summer death for the green birch/pine forest of northern WI—Camp Timberlane—to be exact. Yep, Camp Counselor Jack, that's me—for the summer anyway. I really didn't want to stay down here for the summer—just too damn hot. I should have looked for a job in or near Flagstaff since it is still "away from home" and in the mountains. O-well, maybe the autumn will find me there.

I do have reservations about going back to the state of WI, but at least I'll still be hours away from La Crosse. Actually, I'll probably spend a couple weeks (on and off) there in LaX before my time at camp will start. Yes, I'm nervous/anxious (anxiety kills) to see what it'll be like. Actually, I may be a bit more anxious to look into those surroundings and see/feel the ghost of my former self. A self that once lived manipulated and in fear of the dawn and dusk that turned every day into another night of hell in life. I have been gearing up for the return. I figure: <u>Fuck. Everyone. Else</u>. I'm living for me now. I won't be manipulated—I won't let someone else's fucked up view of the world sucker me into compassion for their neurosis/psychosis. And I'm not talking about Susan. I'm talking about that twisted fuck who stalked and terroristically taunted both Susan and me in those final weeks of that hell. I honestly don't want to confront my (former) friend Tim. I don't know how/if I would handle it. I think it wouldn't take much to spark me off. Like tossing a match into a powder keg. I'm still pissed but would rather not confront him and let it fizzle out than to confront him and risk losing my mind and becoming physically aggressive. He may be bigger than me, but I think I am a lot more pissed off. A lot more.

So anyway, I'm going to spend some quality time with my good friends and not let the existence of those other people bring me down. One thing that does get me sad is knowing that even though you're six hours away, I could be there in just that time if I felt like it. I mean, I felt (feel) better knowing a good friend is within driving distance. I'm gonna miss you even more now. Although I don't leave until mid May so if you want to fly over, I would love to see you. If you do, bring your tent so we can go camping up in the mountains. Damn right. Back to natural wonder and real majesty.

Lately, I've been listening to a lot of Brother Ray (Charles). I'm glad to hear you're finding peace in music—Johnny D. He always reminds me of my mom—she used to listen to him (a lot) when I was growing up. Good stuff.

I'm sorry to hear Lana is going through the problems that she is. Sorrows can be drowned in drugs. They can also die. I hope she sees that it is a dead end road and that there are better ways to deal with pain (isn't that why people abuse drugs? To numb how they feel inside? I think so).

How's your new roomie situation going? Friends can be friends, but roommates can get on one's nerves—and lovers as well. Just be careful not to ruin a friendship over the trifles of sharing a bathroom—or a bed. Look out for numero uno. You have to be selfish sometimes, you know. I hope it turns out well. Hey if you come visit, I'll let you go through my closet and pick some clothes you like— my condolences on your lost clothing. That really sucks. If you find the person who took them, make them strip down to their undies.

What have you been reading lately? I picked up *The Outsider* by Richard Wright. It's a pretty philosophical (existentialist) book that looks good. I haven't finished reading a bunch of the other books I'm reading, but I'm working on it, you know.

I've been waiting to tell you about me moving cause I sort of feel good and bad about it. I mean, it isn't like I'm going back home, not really, but it sort of is (and gives me that "failure" feeling—like I couldn't handle it away and therefore need to go back). But I really don't expect or plan on being there past

September. Maybe something cool will come up. I definitely want to come back out west again, not sure where though. Maybe Utah, but maybe I'll come back to AZ—maybe Flagstaff, maybe SD. Who knows?! I don't. But I have faith that my path will be lit as I move along. I want, most definitely, to stay in touch with my number one letter-writing pal—YOU—in case I have an itch to go straight out to Cali come the wintertime. You are my southern Cal connection. Bueno? I'm sure we'll discuss it as time passes.

It's 4:40 AM, and I am dazing off almost regularly. No one on the day shift has bothered to remember to get some coffee for us lowly freaks of the nightshift. Have I mentioned how discontented I am with these hours? Yeah, probably. My mind is thick with sleepiness, and when I get back home in 2½ hours, I probably won't be sleepy anymore. I haven't slept three nights in a row in about 6 months. That sucks ass.

My folks will be here on Tuesday. My mom is bringing down my typewriter so maybe I'll type a letter or two.

Did I tell you, I went out and purchased (again) that same Sinead disk that you picked up? Sinead O'rtega! I was reminded of how good it was after you played it and I couldn't get some of those tracks out of my mind. Jessie and I have both been enjoying it regularly.

So, I've been priming myself for a summer at camp by tanning my skin slowly but surely. I couldn't possibly return after 9 months in AZ and not have color in my skin. I am jealous that you're surfing—bastard! I think that would be shitloads of fun once you got the hang of it. If you're still considering moving into the mountains, maybe in the fall I'll hunt you down and live, who knows, but keep me in mind—I've got you there (in my mind).

Go get yourself some nature, remember what you're missing. Life doesn't exist in urbanity, only existence is there. Life exists, as does existence, in Nature. Or just come here to visit.

I hope everything is going well with you and Ted and Lana. I think about you often. Write or call me if you plan to visit. So, until then, go sit under a palm tree and let the warm southern California sun beat down on you and fill you with strong positive (+) energy. I'll talk to you soon.

Miss you too, Brother.
Jackson.

35.
Hello JT,

If you ever type a letter to me, I'll hit you. If you want to be impersonal, I'll hook you up with a few learning sessions with Ted.

Everything is fine here. Living situation is quite interesting so far in the first few days. I'll keep you posted. I am currently searching for guidance with a few things in my life. One issue being that of why—no—what (first of all) my feelings are toward my new roommate. I love him, of course, but I'm starting to think that I've been denying the fact that I'm IN love with him. I think, without guidance, being his roommate will drive me cruelly insane—with jealousy. I've just begun looking into <u>intuition</u> and what it can mean and lead to if followed and also what it can teach you. We'll see if it leads to having some questions answered. It's totally nice having my own bedroom though!

The next question I need answered is why on earth or in the heavens do I have these feelings for him anyway, and why can I not seem to rid myself of them no matter how hard I try? Maybe I just need to meet someone else to cast my affection onto. If Ted's not going to be receptive to it, then fuck him.

Ok, let me vent a little more.

So he tells me the other night that he knows what it's like to have sex and now he's taking some time off from it to see what it's like being without sex for a while and to try to gain a "closer to Krishna consciousness." He says he doesn't want to "spill seed" (which sort of reminds me of that "Every Sperm is Sacred" song from Monty Python's *The Meaning of Life*, remember that?). Well, that's all fine and dandy with me cuz I can live with my hand—speaking of the meaning of life...ugh. We need to revisit that topic some time.

Anyways, the first two nights in our new apartment, we slept together—just slept—which was <u>wonderful</u>, just being able to cuddle with someone all night, someone who I wanted to cuddle with. So tonight he's going over to his friend John's house to stay the night—which is fine and dandy because I know there's no relationship going on here. But I do know that everything Ted says about his friend John—it's always about sex. So I confront him on the fact that he said he was going to take some time off from sex. It sort of stopped him into a slight hesitation until he said that John is someone he would consider having a relationship with, and if they had sex, it wouldn't be so bad…

So does that mean that there is nothing in his heart that would have ever driven him to having had sex with me out the possibility for a relationship? Does that mean that all sex between us was to satisfy his need to get off? Here I'm doing it to get closer to him, but he just to make his rocks pop.

I have noticed, however, that he won't kiss me anymore when we do anything. Maybe I should just make it a point never to do anything with him unless I first get the most meaningful of connections—the kiss. Am I grossing you out with all of this? There's just SO MUCH MORE than just sex! Okay, I'll stop. I guess it's his loss, right?

Now I can't wait for Ted to leave tonight—in about 20 minutes—so I can turn on some good music, jam out, write a little more, get naked and play the air guitar—or whatever. Oh, will the problems with roommates ever end? Sigh…

Ok, new topic.

I was packing up to move, and I found my briefcase in the closet—an interesting place to find all my old notebooks, essays, and unedited poems—in the closet!! Anyhow, I took some time off from packing to browse through the stuff. Among the many interesting pieces of writing which reflected the many different periods I've wiggled through in my life, I found our old—on paper, diagrammed conversations we had at the Eagle's Nest. Quite the lucky find! I had thought they were gone. But my point is, through reading my old, unfinished writing, I have realized that maybe I <u>can</u> write. In fact, yeah, I kind of can! You wouldn't have believed how stupid I must have looked dancing around my apartment, laughing, praising the heavens and all of that.

Ted left—my time to shine! So I now feel like my creativity is seeping back into me, gently but surely. (I'm naked already.) I just need to get this apartment in order and sit back during some of my free time and create, create, create!

Oh, what else is going on in my life? Since I've been feeling so inadequate lately, I decided to go to the foundation upon which my growth began—*The Celestine Prophesy*. Ben, my old roommate's boyfriend in La Crosse, borrowed my old copy and never gave it back to me before I left, but just two days ago, I found it at this kickass used bookstore two blocks from my house—just a little hole in the wall on the outside, but on the inside, an abundance of treasures. I'm talking spiritual, psychology and metaphysical books from the way-early 1900's for cheap.

"Bow Down Mister" by Boy George is a pretty cool song by the way.

What have I been reading, you ask? I recently finished Carlos Casteneda's *The Art of Dreaming*—interesting, in depth, kind of odd book about entities he came into touch with through dreaming. And I just finished *The Book—On the Taboo Against Knowing Who You Are,* by Alan Watts. I went into the Blue Door Bookstore and told the clerk there, Phil, that I needed something to uplift my spiritual depression, and he suggested this book by Alan Watts—he said he used to use it as a textbook when he was a teacher. The fucking book completely sucked. Talk about a guy with no more than a linear mind! He used all these great examples in order to get the reader to understand his point of view—which I've discovered the only thing he's good at is logic—with his scientific, needing to be proven to be true, mind. Basically everything this 170 page book had to say went completely against what I believe—except for the idea that our bodies are only of this earth. But he also thinks our minds—essentially our souls—are only of this earth too—at least that's what I got out of it (and maybe I totally missed the point). He says that when we die, that's it—period. Sorry, but I believe that every life is a learning process, and we have specific things to learn in each life we live—and yes, we live many more than just one life. Don't you think that's nice of that Phil guy at the bookstore though? Yep, I'm searching for a book to help my soul—to lift my spirits in a sense—and he tells me to read this book that says, "We're all just gonna die!" Real nice! I'm SO uplifted! Maybe I just didn't "get it." Who knows… So now I'm reading a book about channeling, which I also picked up from that cool used bookstore. So far, it has been completely complementing my toddler beliefs and has me screaming, "More frosting. More frosting!" I kind of want to know a little about some of my past lives—am I weirding you out?

Your job sounds like a dream-come-true. It's something I've always wanted to do—not your job now I mean, but your soon-to-be summer job. I want to make it out before you go, but I don't know when I'm going to see money from Lana yet, or if I ever will. If I don't see it soon, however, I will be calling her mother and saying something like, "Could you call your daughter and remind her that age-old rent bills come before drugs?"

I have "Bow Down Mister—Hare Rama, Hare Krishna"—on repeat and am probably annoying the few neighbors we have—cool ones though. Ted's been gone 50 minutes now, and I'm still not dancing around yet. Maybe I'll say something to Ted like, "I realize what I have in you when you're not here, and I love it. But when I'm around you, I just want to put my arms around you and squeeze—until the time inevitably comes when you make me jealous."

134

By the way, I did meet someone, and let me use this as an example to epitomize my relationship with Ted. So I meet this cute Mexican guy at Thrify. I ask him to come up to my apartment for a beer and so he does. We chat, get to know each other, become friends. So one day we go to pick him up so he can come along with Lana and me and Ted while we take Ted to the Krishna temple in PB. But when Ernesto approaches the car, Ted sees him and says, "Oh that queen?" To make a short story shorter, a week later Ted sleeps with him, and then I never (nor Ted) hear from Ernesto again. So, in essence, since Ernesto knew Ted is my best San Diegan friend, he was embarrassed that he slept with him and now won't talk to me again.

In fact, I saw Ernesto from a distance the other day—I waved, and he just kept walking. So, basically, Ted and his ways destroyed a friendship, but I won't say that. I'm not that evil. Could it be that I'm a little too forgiving? Tell me damn it! Give me the news. I can take it!

So I write, bitch, and moan about all of this and diss Ted here and there, but he certainly does have a warm side. He told me about his best friend who recently died of cancer (before I moved here). He was a pre-devotee, planning to give himself to the Hindu monkhood upon successfully beating the cancer. Well, that didn't happen. Ted told me that the last thing his friend said to his mother before he died was, "I am OM." Then at the funeral, his mom said she had seen an OM form in the clouds that morning. Hmm. Ted now teeters on the edge of

135

devotee-ism (I believe you knew that). He wants me to get a tattoo of an OM with him. It would probably be a better decision going with an OM on my forearm rather than a giant penis, eh? Not sure though—your butt cheek looks good and all (and Ted's arm healed great!), but I'm still not sold on tats.

Okay, enough! I'll bitch to you more later.

Love and Spirit,
Marc.

36.
Marcky-Marc,

Ohh, I don't believe I can express the discontent I feel with these hours I work. Less than a month to go, but every night feels like an eternity. I am presently at work, 1:57 AM 4/10/96.

Let me tell you I am <u>very excited</u> to have you come visit. I need to get out and back to some nature (although I'm sure I'll have plenty of it this summer). I'm glad this will be SW nature though. I sort of like the desert, although it sucks for biking. It can be beautiful and very hostile at once. I am in great anticipation of our wild adventure to the south.

I hope everything is going better with the living situation. It can get complicated, huh? Especially when romantic and/or sexual circumstances mix with the regular stresses of living with someone. I'm sure if Jessie and I were "involved," it would be hell. I agree that if Ted isn't going to be receptive to you to the extent you feel is respectful, then it's his loss. You need to retain self respect and demand respect from him if there is to be success—as far as my opinion goes anyway. Perhaps getting a tattoo together would be a nice bonding experience. You could get locking OM's... how cute!

I could tell you were stressed because your handwriting got more erratic as the words went by (damn handwriting giving secrets away).

You brought up kissing and its correlation to meaningful connections. I believe that's why most prostitutes don't kiss their clients—it's too personal. It gets too easy to become emotionally involved, not just physically—make sense?

I'm glad to hear you've found some of your old writing, not to mention that which evolved from our class skipping Friday afternoon writing times, sipping beers and eating popcorn at the Eagles Nest. I still have those notes too.

Yes, you can write. Yes you can.

I must admit, I have become less pragmatic since discovering a more spiritual side of life. By spiritual, I mean Buddhist and Taoist philosophies as well as the connections I've made (however deep or superficial) with my own soul.

So how does one meet someone at the market and end up having him coming up to the apartment for a beer? You must have something, right?

My, my, my. Three weeks from yesterday, you'll be in Tucson, and three weeks from today, we'll be on our way south to Patagonia—damn near Mexico!—to exist naturally for three days in nature. Do you have a sleeping pad or mattress for camping? If not, you may want to bring an extra blanket(s) to sleep on because I don't have a pad so my two blankets will go under _my_ body. There isn't much soft soil, grass or anything the body really prefers to sleep upon around here.

I hope everything is going well, and I want to say, again, that I'm _really_ looking forward to your visit. It'll be much needed. Take care of yourself. Watch out for number 1. I got the freight train blues.

Peace.
Jackson.

37.
Jack the Man,

I can imagine how the women must strip off each layer in that Arizona heat. Yes, the erratic handwriting may have been sexual deprivation; however, it could also have been cuz I was getting pretty loaded on beer and the thoughts were flowing Jack K. style. I am extremely looking forward to two weeks from Tuesday and am in desperate need for a little R&R&H&C (hikin' and

138

campin'). I will bring a sleeping pad. It will be much easier now that you've got a tent and I don't have to lug mine around.

I have today off work—a lazy one it's been. I took a couple walks and stopped at a few bookstores—new and used—just to browse though since I'm broke until payday. I'm averaging about 35 hours at Tribeans—which is perfect. And if I keep living a life of simple pleasures—a little tv, lots of tea, and plenty of reading (maybe I'll try to weave some writing in there too), I should make it okay with one job for the meantime.

I re-read *The Celestine Prophecy*, read a foundational book about channeling, and just finished *Way of the Peaceful Warrior* by Dan Millman (what a wonderfully heartwarming, mind-forgetting—mind opening—read!) which made my eyes water with (mostly) joy. After each metaphysical and/or soul-searching book I've read, I've immediately found myself in the bookstore looking for another to try to pry my eyes open even wider, until I put down Millman's book. It seems to be just perfect, just enough for me to understand what I need in my life for right now—balance—and an understanding that it will all work out if I put my mind to things and not worry about little moments or hiccups in my life.

Today, I found myself looking at gay fiction—which I've never really been interested in. I guess my quest for spiritual truth has subsided for the moment. Perhaps Millman's novel held the keys that fit all the right locks for me right now, though who knows how long it will last.

I'm just sort of going with the flow. I feel like a carrot ready to be pulled from the ground, but nothing's going to pull me except for the sun—that bright white light that feeds energy to all that is—wow, sounds mystical, eh? Perhaps a bit cliché…

I'm sitting at Panikin now, just ordered some Garden Treat tea (herbal, wonderful). I feel pretty good. I just went to the Juice Club and gave Alien Joe (remember him?) a big hug and a smile—just for the heck of it. I know where he works and he knows where I work—that's it. No addresses or phone numbers anymore so I never see him. He came into my work about two weeks ago, handed me a rose, and walked out. Didn't buy coffee or nothing. I haven't seen or talked to him since then so I decided to do this for him tonight. I hope it made him feel good—it made me feel better. Sometimes the simplest things—at first so hard to do—prove to be so worthwhile. Whether it be a simple hug or the utterance of a two-syllable word which can mean so much and be so liberating—"Goodbye"—the freedom one can receive, from pain or from guilt, can be extraordinary.

I also told him I love him, and he returned the comment. Just knowing that he cares and that he thinks about me (the rose) means so much.

With simple things, such as the knowledge of something like this off my mind and out of my subconscious (from taking two minutes out of my day), it seems that my body and soul are able to soar more gently through the world. And perhaps I will see my art of writing return more quickly if I continue doing things I want to do but have been too afraid to. This would mean, then, that I would also be lifted to the higher spiritual realms (higher vibrations) that exist within and all around the things of this earth. I would not be stuck to the mechanics of our physical existence, which would be highly liberating (not being stuck in the muck, that is). Too bad if I sound a little nutty—perhaps it's that channeling book affecting me. My mother should hear me now!

So anyway, Ted has now joined me for tea.

Holy shit! He just showed me his new tattoo! He got his OM! (without me—which is fine). It's in Devanagari script, about 4 inches wide, and it's WAY cool!

It's a few days later and day two of not smoking. It's difficult to not raise my voice about a lot of things, but I'm coping so far. There's a huge silver-dollar-sized cockroach in our pantry. Yuck. I think I've decided that when I get enough money saved up, I'm going to move again. I used one of Ted's pans to cook some eggs the other day—Ted's a vegetarian—lacto-ovo, ish—it's not the eggs that freaked him out—it's that I used butter to cook them in rather than ghee. He said his pan was ruined now that the disgusting, unclarified butter had touched it. He was seriously bitching at me about it! I told him I'd just wash it and to relax, but he kept bitching, said it didn't matter, it couldn't be washed now, it was just ruined. Interestingly, he used it to make his dal in later that same night!

I'm thinking Santa Fe—possibly August 1 or so. What do you think? I'm going to just quit now and mail this tomorrow and give my brain a chance to get used to all the O2 it's been receiving lately.

Talk to you soon.
Marcc (with two C's)

Marc's vacation finally arrived. He and Jack drove to Patagonia State Park, 80 miles south of Tucson, and circled the camping area looking for a shaded site to set up camp. Although it was early spring, the southern Arizona sun baked the cacti shadows to the dry stones.

The best sites were already occupied. Shade was difficult to find in the remaining area of the park, and what shade existed was just a few lightly foliaged mesquite trees. Settling for one of the few sites remaining, the two snuggled the tent up close to a bush-sized tree hoping for at least some sort of protection from the hot afternoon sun.

A cold beer helped cool them down and a blanket served as a seating area near the fire pit, the cooler close at hand, the picnic table pulled near for use as a countertop for empty beer bottles and a loaf of bread. A few pieces of fruit and Marc's homemade hummus beckoned flies to the plastic grocery bag.

When they finished arranging the site to their satisfaction, they strolled a quarter mile to the cold lake to take a dip. JT had brought his Frisbee, which they tossed around as they waded up to their ankles in the icy water.

Parched, the Frisbee game didn't last long as the resistance of the water proved to be too much effort in the southern sun.

As the evening wore on and the desert air began to cool, a few beers were washed down with Funyuns and Chex Mix hors d'oeuvres. Jack built the fire and tossed foil-wrapped fajitas and potatoes onto the glowing coals. The night consisted of their usual consumption of beers and great conversation, as though they had never been apart.

Jack awoke early the next morning and carried his backpack out of the tent. Marc joined him when the temperature inside the tent rose to unbearable from the direct rays of the rising sun. Jack's notebook rested on the picnic table, supporting his arm and a pen. He had been writing while the water for his instant coffee heated over the fire. When Marc emerged from the tent, Jack gently folded the cover of his notebook and placed it and his pen aside.

Marc noticed and asked him what he had been writing about, but Jack just shrugged, then swirled some water around in his coffee mug and tossed it out onto the dirt beside him. Marc figured he'd give him some time to finish. He pulled his coffee tote from his bag, poured in some water from the teapot before it had begun to whistle, scooped a tablespoon of instant coffee into his mug, and walked away into the hills surrounding them.

Jack took note of Marc's kindness, *like his gesture to Alien Joe,* he thought, then opened his notebook again and continued his writing.

Marc looked all around him, taking in the sea of small trees that surrounded the cliff where he sat. He began to think about how trees forgive human beings, how they dedicate their lives to working for them. When humans invade their space, when we remove the trees from their habitats, when they've completed their work, having fed us

143

oxygen from their first days until their deaths, they continue to protect us, providing shelter and heat. In a sense, they exist to appease us during and after their lives.

Marc stared at a small bug that landed on his fingertip, watched it crawl around the underside of his hand as if it were hiding. A small cactus hid under the shade of a young tree. At that moment, Marc felt as if he were that cactus. He wondered what Jack had been writing.

When Marc returned to the campsite, Jack's notebook was closed and his guitar was on his knee.

"What do you say we take a little hike," Marc suggested.

"I'm up for it," said Jack. "I heard there's an area just south of the lake where we might find some geodes."

They packed their backpacks full with water bottles and a few sandwiches, and Jack snapped the last of the film remaining in his camera and reloaded another roll. They stopped at the campground manager's office and asked the dark-skinned woman if she knew the route to the geodes.

"Ah hear they fond some-a-them things down near the ol' quarry south-a-the dam," she answered in a southern-style accent, like she'd been transplanted from the Smoky Mountains.

"Thank you, ma'am," Jack said with southern charm. Though he wasn't southern, Jack had mastered the mimicking of accents that nobody knew existed, and he charmed everyone they encountered, including Marc.

They followed the directions the woman had given and reached the dam easily. There, they stopped for a drink of water, already warm in their backpacks. The river water rushed through the sluice below. It looked clean and cold, and it attracted them. Above the dam, the river was thin and the land was cut, corroded by the river. Dunes of dried mud cracked in the heat.

They followed the river south, sometimes sliding down the slick, hard mud and dipping a foot into the river water. It was still a long walk to the old quarry, but they were determined to find a souvenir.

Jack led the way as Marc followed closely behind. Jack's bare back and legs glistened in the sun, his shirt tucked into the side of his shorts, hanging loosely against his right leg. His Yin/Yang peeked out of his waistline. He moved like a dancer, not flamboyant, but smooth and graceful. His body seemed to transform in front of Marc's eyes. He was controlled, captivated, engrossed by Jack's beauty.

Marc shook his head, trying to release the thoughts. "I need to stop for some water," he said.

An hour later, they arrived at the old quarry decaying on the western slope of the large canyon into which they had descended.

Before they began their hunt for geodes, Jack found a flat rock, placed his camera upon it, and set the timer for a snapshot.

Perhaps they found geodes that day, perhaps not. The attempts to break open any of the possibilities they had found proved futile. Any beauty the stones may have held remained hidden inside.

Before long, the sun sank to 2 PM. The sweat began drying white on their foreheads and their knees became slightly shaky. Though their drinking water ran low, they didn't risk filling up with the trickling desert water.

Jack put his shirt on. Although he'd been slowly preparing his skin for his return back to Wisconsin, the sun won this round. He snapped a couple pictures of Marc against the backdrop of ocotillo-laced dry hills and dirt, and they were on their way back to camp, if they could find it.

At the dam, they stared at each other, their fingertips digging into their skulls—neither could remember where the main path was. The heat of the long day wore on their minds as well as their bodies.

"Well it can't be that way," said Marc pointing up the trail that led away from the setting sun.

"Okay," agreed Jack. "Camp's north. Let's stick to the north trail."

They continued, but when the trail narrowed, they both knew they had chosen wrong. Prickers from waste-high bushes dug into their legs while their bodies continued to bake in the sun. They accused each other only briefly.

"Marc, you know it's just the heat talking. Let's just turn around."

"But we're already fifteen minutes into this trail. Turning back would add another half hour to this stupid hike. Besides, the lake's just up ahead. Maybe we can walk along the shore back to camp."

"I guess so," said Jack.

A bit further up they came upon a larger path. Relieved for the moment, they stopped to pick the fuzzy little stickers from the sleeves of their t-shirts, the burrs off their socks, and the thorns out of their thighs. They were hopeful that the larger path would lead them back to camp.

The trail quickly led them down a steep slope to the edge of the water. Broken glass and a small fire pit in the sand told them stories of drunken privacy seekers, though they were the only ones there at the moment.

The lake reached into the shoreline forming a lagoon. The short trees grew into a thick forest of prickers to the edge of the shore. Scanning the area, hopeful to find a path that circled the lagoon, they realized they were at the end of the only path available.

Jack recognized the area on the other side of the lagoon, which rested about 30 yards from the south shore they stood upon. He was sure of it. They had a decision to make: climb back up the steep slope and look for another path around the lagoon, or take a plunge and swim to the north shore. Although they had their backpacks and Jack had his camera, they agreed a swim would be a refreshing end to their long day.

Jack was protective of his photos, his memories, and he asked Marc to take his backpack so he could carry the camera alone. Rolled up, the backpack fit nicely inside Marc's.

They waded into the water, holding their goods above their heads. The water was cold, very cold on such a hot desert day—the contrast shocked them. The lake deepened quickly and they were soon swimming, each of them with a hand high above the water holding the camera, wallets, notebooks.

The lake water refreshed them in a way, though icy cold, but they were weak from the long day. Jack began hyperventilating as he lost power in his legs. To their left, the horizon was bright orange as the sun set. Marc swam faster than Jack until he looked back and saw him struggling.

"Are you okay?" Marc shouted, treading water with his legs and right arm. Jack couldn't answer. Marc swam faster toward the other shore.

"Hel…" he heard quietly over the splashing water.

Marc looked back again. Jack wasn't swimming anymore. He struggled to keep his head above water, but his mouth and nose bobbed below the surface—he was determined to keep the camera dry.

"Do you need me?" Marc yelled. He didn't know what to do. Was Jack really in that much trouble? Should he

147

save the notebooks and wallets that were in the backpacks first?

"Help me," Marc heard, Jack's voice clear but strained. Marc heaved the backpacks, hoping they'd hit dirt, and swam back out toward Jack. He could only see the top of JT's head and his hand that held the camera above the water. Marc pulled him up and grabbed the camera out of his hand.

"I've got the camera," Marc said.

Jack began swimming again, slowly, using both arms. "My legs are gone," he said.

"Can you stay above water?" Marc yelled to him, already swimming back to shore, "or should I lose the camera?"

"No, don't. I'm okay."

Marc swam to shore as Jack languished behind, though his second arm proved quite valuable in keeping him afloat. They were exhausted, sunburned, and ready for beers. They lay upon the shore as the horizon swallowed the remaining sun.

Twilight swarmed them. Marc rustled first, sitting up and brushing off the dirt that had dried to his arms as the moisture evaporated from them.

"We may need to camp here tonight," he admitted, not knowing whether Jack was listening or asleep.

"I'm cool with that," responded Jack, surprising Marc with his lingering sense of humor. He sat up, began brushing at his arms as Marc had done. "You saved my life, man," he said, reflecting.

"Fuck you," Marc spit out. "You weren't in _that_ much trouble," he teased.

"My fuckin' nose was under!"

"Seriously? Why didn't you lose the camera then?"

"No idea," Jack admitted. "Stubborn."

148

With that, a short, choked giggle escaped each of their throats.

"I'm not sleeping here," said Jack. "I need a beer, damn it."

"Well, my legs are all beat up already anyways. Let's keep making trails."

They followed the shore another twenty minutes until they saw the lights from their campground. After a long, long day, it was time to camp.

Unfortunately for Jack, his tough hike wasn't quite over. Later that year, way up at Camp Timberlane in the north woods of Wisconsin, Jack would show me a picture of himself, a look of despair despite the twinkle in his eyes. He was shirtless, a sweat-stained red bandana tied around his neck and a big red sore on his forehead from a low-hanging tree limb he'd smacked into just as he and Marc arrived back at camp.

"Perfect," he thought. "Just perfect."

38.
June 2, 1996
Marc,

Well, it has been mostly cloudy in WI since we've been back, but I'm having a good time anyway. Hopefully this pseudo-spring will be over soon and summer will shine. I go up north to Camp Timberlane in a week, so right now it's all like a vacation. Been playing guitar regularly and getting drunk (on the cheap!) at the Popcorn on a regular basis. I saw an old friend Quinn there last night and showed him my Yin/Yang. He got all excited about it (surprised that I finally got my first tat). He's been an artist for a few years and is trying to convince me

149

to let him give me another. Perhaps it's time to get that penis on my forearm? I should probably wait until after my camp counselor experience though.

I've been putting a lot of thought into where I'll go in the fall. I still don't quite know. Very possibly back to Tucson, maybe Santa Fe, or even San Diego.

I picked up *The Beat Reader* by Anne Charters. It should be good summer north-woods reading, no?

How's the personal relation side of life? All good I hope. I've been staying relatively uncommitted and trying to be carefree. It's mostly working. I've been talking to my friend/ex-roommate Damon lately— he spent a few months last year in Chiapas, Mexico. We've been discussing the possibility of life in Mexico—on a longer-term timeline, like in two years. A lot of logistical and financial planning would be involved. But it's all talk now—who knows where we'll be in two years. I sure would like to gain some of that cultural experience though, not to mention really learn Spanish.

How's Tribeans? Good I hope. Still smoking? I'll hope not, but I can't say much since I still have one occasionally.

Not much to report here. I just wanted to get a note out to you to make sure you have my summer address and this picture that was saved by YOU— thanks again! What the fuck is that by the way? A halo? Your aura? Water-damage to the film?

Please write me at least once this summer to let me know how things are going.

Stay up, be good, send a picture.
Peace and Love,
Jack.

39.
JT,

I was relieved to hear from you. I was becoming a little worried that you didn't make it back in one piece. Did you make it to Box Canyon on your way? How's the job? How's the female staff? Are they keeping you busy? You know I am a constant advocate for penises on forearms. But if you don't have the courage, I will understand and be completely happy with an OM.

I had an interesting surprise when I returned back to San Diego. Remember me talking about Jason, the recovering narcotics addict? Well, when I got back, he was nowhere to be found. Turned out he "relapsed" into a nice 3-4 day crystal meth haze (hanging out at the bathhouse the whole time). I tried to be "supportive" so I stuck around hoping he could clean up and get through it, but other recovering people from his NA groups (Narcotics Anonymous—I had gotten to know quite a few of them from hanging out with Jason), they told me that the brain is still not quite right for a few months after the relapse, and finally after about 3 weeks of being extremely patient, I learned he was seeing two other guys as well as me—hmm.

That was that—I said goodbye.

I keep wondering why there's so much addiction among the gay community? Why so much drug use? I know that Lana had a tough upbringing. I remember her dad saying to her once, "Damn your dumb." We all laughed at the time—my brother and sister and me and Lana and her brother—but looking back, holy shit, how often did he say stuff like that to her? It <u>had</u> to have an enormous effect on her—her self worth and shit. And now she's an addict…

Not sure if it's a lack of self worth in the gay guys I know here or if it's just that there're so many drugs here on the west coast. Probably mostly a lack of self worth, I'm guessing, from growing up hearing that gay is bad, that they're not normal, that they're going to Hell. I can't believe how other people's "opinions" and words can affect us so much—I'm forced to reflect on how much other people have probably affected me.

I think about how nice Lana is—how loving she is—how trusting—how she looks past (accepts, actually) any and all differences in others. It makes me wonder if the soft-hearted (the lovers and not the fighters) are more affected by the harsh words of others. It's almost a liberal—conservative thing, it seems. I wonder how many dreams or future goals have been crushed by some asshole trying to control someone else or forcing an opinion on them…

These are the folks that turn to drugs, among other things. They're some of the nicest ones and the ones who are therefore affected by how others view them. They try to please others—they want to "smooth things out" all the time. And isn't it better that way?

Yet the "controlling" ones always seem to win—the ones who control with words or violence—it's not right. Gay or straight, black or white, words of judgment and negativity breed oppression, right? Lana was probably so affected by her dad's comments (and whatever else) that she tries to drown her feelings in whatever way she can.

Now imagine Jason and other gay people. I know, obviously, that coming out is horribly difficult and that people hear such negative things about homosexuality everywhere they go—starting in school, then church, then many homes and among friends a lot of the time—I don't have to tell you it's rough. Did you know some parents kick their kids out of the house because they're gay? It apparently happens more often than one would think, and there are shelters out there that are specifically for gay homeless kids. I don't get it. Shouldn't it be illegal to kick your underage kids out of your house? Shouldn't those parents be arrested for neglect or emotional abuse or both? Thinking about it, shouldn't parents be arrested for emotional abuse when they put their kids through that gay therapy crap? They remove kids from their homes when their parents abuse them, so shouldn't teaching them that gay is bad, especially when a kid might be gay, be considered abuse? It's almost like raising a blond child and calling her stupid all her life because she has blond hair. Wouldn't that be emotional or psychological abuse?

I remember I asked my mom once what she'd do if I brought a black girl home. She said, "I'd probably disown you." When I look back on it, holy shit (again), I can't believe she would say that to her teenage son! It's a good thing I didn't come to terms with being gay until college, otherwise I might have been homeless too, out on the streets just like that, for loving who I love. I should've known all along how she would react to me being gay, now that I remember her opinion of mixing races. Where the hell did she get those opinions anyway? Her own sister married a Mexican guy, and she hasn't disowned her!! I guess she feels her only option (or hope) at getting her way anymore is by instilling fear—do this and I'll disown you—do that and you're going to hell—it never ends, you know?

Anyways, it's no wonder so many gay people are on drugs. Generally sensitive and loving individuals dramatically affected by some controlling, sorry-asses of human beings.

Hey, thanks for the rant. It was a sad day letting go of Jason. I remember walking home from North Park back to Hillcrest listening to the Greatest Hits of George Jones, and of course the song I kept rewinding the most was "He Stopped Loving Her Today." Stupid song.

So then a day later, I went on a date with this guy—he wanted to take me to dinner. I told him up front that I'm a vegetarian and he said, "no problem," but he still took me to this steak joint. I kept reminding him that I'm a vegetarian, and he kept saying, "no problem." Then he orders two meals like I was the silent partner, like I was his lady and he was doing me a favor, being chivalrous or something—so I was like *whatever*—and I just decided to see what he had up his sleeve—maybe he knew something I didn't... So, the meals come and—you're going to love this—he stabs the chicken breast from my plate and puts it on his, then dumps the vegetables from his plate onto mine and goes on eating like it's all fine and dandy! Un-fucking real!

So, then the next day—so much action, I know—I was at work and this guy comes in and starts talking to me. I remembered him from a week before when he came into Tribeans basically holding his wiener cuz he had to pee so bad. So we chatted for about 15 minutes (after he peed), and I asked him out for coffee the next day. Turns out he'd been coming into Tribeans for the past month just to see me—ha! We had coffee, went to dinner, then a movie. We got along fabulously. It was THE best date I've ever been on.

At the movie theater, they have those seats where you pull down the armrests. The one between us was up, and as the movie progressed, our elbows touched, then our pinkies touched, then his hand was on top of mine, and finally we were holding hands. It was just like high school! He dropped me off after a 7-hour date (by the way, I couldn't tell you how the movie was).

The next day Scott took me to see the sea lions that lay on the beach in La Jolla, and Friday I went to LA with him and stayed at his parents' house until Monday. Our first kiss was that Friday night on Santa Monica Blvd. in West Hollywood at a coffee shop where Barbara Streisand was singing "People" through the speakers.

Anyhow, the valerian tea is kicking in so…

Okay I'm back. It's a couple days later, and I'm sitting with Scott now at Balboa Park—he's sunning—I'm writing, though I'm not going to write too much since he's here.

I moved out of Ted's. He was becoming a little nutty (a little?). Anyhow, we both thought it was best if I moved on. So I've been staying with my friend Bobby a couple miles down the road toward downtown. His apartment is right below the flight path of landing airplanes. We're watching TV and suddenly can't hear a damn thing while a plane is passing over. It's a small studio, and I've had the couch. Last night we listened to Priscilla, Queen of the Desert's "Hey Lady" like a hundred times. Bobby's hilarious. I think you met him—Tribeans, redhead, Mr. Heat-Miser?!

Anyhow, Scott's been talking about possibly moving back to LA, and it sounds like he wants me to move there with him. Tell you what, the way I'm feeling right now has me saying, yep, let's do it. I could easily transfer to a Tribeans there. I know there's a possibility that you could be moving here, right? Well, if it happens, it's only a couple hours away, and we could always spend weekends hanging out. I guess I am at rock bottom (financially for sure) so I can only go up from here, right? We'll see.

I have to learn my coffee families in the next couple days to get a whopping 15 cent raise—yee haa.

So, I hope everything is going great.

Miss you much, and keep lovin' the alligators!
Marc.

40.
Howdy Jackson,

I know you're busy and are probably not getting time to write many letters while you're counseling kids up there in Wisconsin, so I'll just keep writing. I know that's what you would do.

I've been thinking a lot lately. Have you ever felt like you want to take an intriguing path somewhere you've never experienced before, but when your mind starts acting up, you feel like a big dark hand keeps smacking you on the face or any other part of your body that is close to finding a grasp on that trail? Perhaps all I've got to do is jab a little and shed a little tear on both sides and get on down the path.

Is it good (or even okay) to shed the human compassion thing for a moment—maybe a couple months? Is it okay to focus on me—just me—for a while and become a rock when others may be hurt in the process? Is it even possible to guarantee—or promise—more happiness after a period of hurt? Would it be lying to them? Would I be fooling both myself and others? Or am I just afraid? How long and what is it going to take to find out who I am? What the hell is in store for me and when am I going to discover it? Is doing something "crazy" also considered to be doing something "stupid"?

How come I can feel so secure and happy sometimes in my life and yet feel so unbalanced, depressed and stuck at other times even though my situation hasn't changed a single bit? Perhaps it's the constant barrage of negativity I get from the Madre. I spoke with her briefly about a week ago, and after about 8 and a half minutes of listening to her talk about her life, she told me yet again that I have to give my life to Jesus, reminded me that only those filled with the Holy Spirit will make it into Heaven. I sort of didn't have the patience for that at the time so I asked her about the Buddhists and all the starving African children, told her again to read some books other than the Bible, and then hung up.

Well, it didn't take her long to get back to me. Here's a quote from her letter I received yesterday: "Marcus, The Bible tells us it is inspired by God. God chose the people he wanted to write it and told them what to write. It also tells us that in the end times people will be deceived and led astray by evil men. Marcus the Bible has been around for thousands of years. It is meant to save us and protect us, but we have to follow its principles. I have heard about the new age beliefs and it's wrong Marcus, but I can't make you see that. You can't change the Bible to make it what you want. Either you believe the truth or not and God says we all know, but some will be deceived. Just remember, the Holy Spirit is not in everyone, only the ones who believe in Jesus and have been sanctified through him. And only they will be allowed into Heaven, because God will not allow sin into Heaven."

I need to move off grid. Or perhaps I need to spit in her face, steal her sandal, and call her the woman of the unsandaled, like the Bible commands some people to do... Gosh, JT, will this never change?

Actually, my life has changed dramatically since my last letter. The Scott guy suddenly changed to a guy named Gabriel. And, going with the flow of things (and intuition as I've been trying to depend so much on lately), we're already living together. A very sweet and loving man he is, although a little too clingy (touchy-feely). We went up to West Hollywood for LA gay pride, and he wouldn't let go of my arm. The first half hour or so was cool and cute even, but after 5 hours of clinginess, I felt a bit "confined" to say the least. I felt like I needed my space, and I told him so.

Now, my desire to travel—to get out on that intriguing path—is not a result of my new relationship (I don't believe). I've been restless for a long time (as you well know). So, on my path, is Gabriel just helping me along more quickly? (I think the Madre is <u>shoving</u> me along.) I want to go away, but I also want to come back to him. But when I return, will I find him gone?

I just want to travel the country and live for a short time—two weeks or so—in every place I've always wanted to live—Seattle, Colorado, Montana, Santa Fe—take about two months and explore the country and myself.

I'm not formally moving out of San Diego now like I had stated in my last letter—that guy Scott started saying things like, "I don't want you working here or living there." So I said, "Whatever, Becky. See ya!" So now I'm stuck in a year-long lease at this new place—finally away from Ted. I love him (Ted) dearly, but he drives me nuts. (I do miss staying with my friend Bobby, the Heat Miser, though, but his studio was too small.)

My new place is a two bed, two bath, really nice apartment behind the Von's grocery store. So we have an extra bedroom and bath if you need a place to live when you get to San Diego, if you're still coming. I know your life is just as much up in the air as mine is, but keep me informed with your plans.

I have written absolutely nothing lately, but that's okay—I have faith that it (a bestseller) will just pour out of me someday. I guess I'm still thinking positively which is a good thing.

Anyhow, I'm getting tired.

Keep in touch.
Miss you!
Marc.

41.
Dear Friend:

I am not sure if all the questions you've posed to me are meant for me to answer or just for you to vent. I feel like giving some sort of response though. So I will. It seems to me, and many others I've read or heard, that an individual cannot succeed in helping others effectively if they do not first help themselves—or solve their own problems first. I think it is most important—albeit difficult at times—to take time to cure the ills of your own soul before you can expect to be effective in helping others. If your soul is weak, it will only get weaker—eventually breaking down—if neglected. Go ahead, my friend, focus on you. Be the rock you can be. One needs to have happiness to provide happiness, no?

An extended excursion (i.e. two weeks or so in all the places you've wanted to live) sounds like a splendid idea. (Stopping any and all communication with your mother also sounds splendid!)

Until then, don't promise anyone anything! Tell them you will do your best. You know your best is the best—but if you're not at your best, trying to give it will only end up worse—a broken and worn-out soul—in yourself. You know your strengths. I've seen them, heard them, felt them boost my own broken soul. Don't listen to the antiquated (archaic) opinions of your ma. Turn the energy you can generate outwardly into the core of that being that is Marcus Ortega. An OM in your honor, my friend.

I wish I were there to talk with you. It may take a lifetime to find out who you are—but isn't the journey (down the road of self-discovery) the most rewarding part? At least half the fun anyway? I hope you're at least still on the optimist tip. I would be sad to think that things changed—in your mind— to the ugliness of pessimism.

I am not sure where I am going to go come the fall. I would LOVE to go to San Diego, but what kind of work will there be? Do you still have an extra bedroom for me if I come? I am sure I can get a job back in Tucson. I may go back there. I don't really want to—I can't help but think I won't be very happy there. If I do go back, though, I will make the best of it and have a good time—I hope.

Sorry this is so short right now. Find the power, peace, pleasure within you. Stay true to you. Hope is never silent.

Peace and love,
Jackson

Marc,

Sorry I've been sitting on this the last couple weeks, but I'll get it out today. There's only two weeks left of summer camp, then I'm on my way back down to AZ—either Flagstaff or back to Tucson at this point (although a move to San Diego would be awesome).

I want to come out and visit you again. I miss our communication. I've been quite busy up here—too busy sometimes—but will be on the road soon for about a month (through IL, IN, OH, TN, KY, AL, MS, LA, TX, NM, and on to AZ—cool huh). I just hope my car and money hold out through the whole trip.

I'll write more later.

Take care. Follow YOUR way—THE way.
Peace and Love,
JT

41.
Dear Jack,

Gosh, was my last letter that completely depressing? I don't remember being in that bad of condition. But yes, you are absolutely right: Focus on myself and my own soul and sanity before I can let anyone else in.

I am trying once again to quit smoking. I have asked for and am planning on getting a promotion at Tribeans—50 cent raise and more hours—and I joined a gym. So, so far, I've made a pretty good start focusing on myself. Once I have a car, you'll know for sure that I'm doing much better. I feel

163

stuck without a car and will feel much more free with one.

My friends Bobby and Mike and I went camping on a whim the other night. We didn't leave until midnight and finally got set up by 2AM. Perfect sleeping weather, and just like AZ it was 95 degrees by 10 AM. We were packed up and on our way back home to work by 10:30. It was a short trip but well worth it—much needed. I wish I could do that one night each week.

Gabriel and I are getting along quite well—knock on wood—and yes, we still have an extra bedroom if you were to make your way here. It would be good for you to have a job before moving to San Diego if you decided to. However, my personal job searches could only really take place in a very limited area because of my transportation problem. I really don't think you would struggle nearly as much as I did, since you have a car and all.

I like the idea of my mother being antiquated. Perhaps I'll think of her as an antique, as an object that represents a prior era, as a fragile artifact that must be treated with care and caution, or perhaps as a broken piece of used furniture that may be ready to be tossed to the curb...

My horoscope says my creativity will kick in soon again—I can't wait. But until then, I have nothing more to include in this letter except this picture of me and my friend Dean in (sort of) drag—gay pride in Hillcrest—disgusting, huh. Please don't use it as blackmail.

Keep in touch—let me know what's up.
Marcus.

42.
Marco!

Ahh, ready to be in the Southwest again… Dry heat, scrub brush, odd insects and sweet dark-haired beauties. Yes, to be back will be at once a very good feeling and one of "well, I've already 'done this' so why am I here again?" But the second of those would be fruitlessly disappointing to dwell on—so—I am projecting good feelings.

I think of you often and wonder how things are going. Forward progress or nothing I imagine. Yes—that wonderfully enchanting concept of progressive psychosocial progress—but who are we progressing for? Whose measurement of progression and "positive" change are we measuring up to? Hopefully our own, but so many of us, even into adulthood, live in response to social pressures—for society, our friends, our parents (especially), and so many for the church and its conservative values. I think of one of your prior letters discussing the negative aspects or results of not feeling like one is living up to the expectations of others. It is very true. Many of life's "issues" result from the muckiness in one's life—whether it be from the control others attempt to gain or one's desire (need?) to conform to the norms of their community and culture (I again think of weight, fashion, etc.).

But who else is there in the end but ourselves—naked with what integrity we hold as sacred. Will we look back and see that we've lived who we truly were/are? Or will we see a trail of decisions based on fear—my dad wanted me to learn a trade like plumbing, and not be a musician, but thinking for myself, I'd like to move toward the latter. If I do not, won't I regret it? Will I even be happy when my spirit is released from the physical? Only soul is exposed to eternity—we must first progress inside—don't you think—before any truly meaningful positive progressive gains can be made in this commercial, image-conscious (and often soulless), kill or be killed society in which we live, thrive (hopefully), and survive.

It is from this thinking that I allowed my friend Quinn to ink up my physical form. Yes, my body is now home to a new tat—OM! It's not the Devanagari symbol like Ted got—and it's not nearly as big—but I got it on the underside of my left forearm, just the word "OM" about the size of a silver dollar. The craziest shit is that when I was getting it, I was thinking about Ted's OM and then I was thinking about you and about what you have to deal with all the time with your mom, and wondering how you've been, and then in no time Quinn was done. It was hard to see on the underside of my arm so Quinn held a mirror up to it. Well, guess what I read in the mirror. Not OM, but MO!

MO! Marcus Ortega! I've got you forever on my arm, man! Crazy shit! I can't begin to tell you how freaky that is for me—not freaky like because you're on my arm now, but freaky because I'd been thinking about you the whole time Quinn was carving my skin. Just crazy!

It's about a week later, and I am in El Paso Texas as I write this. Not quite to Tucson yet. Hopefully tomorrow we will roll into the great AZ and the grand Sonoran Desert. I'm homeless at this point but don't anticipate a great struggle in finding a place to live. I have a job at the same place I was before—different hours of course! No more awake overnights! I'm moving up! I think everything will be okay as long as my car gets us there.

I left camp on the 12th of August with a fellow counselor named Scott (not your Scott of course—or I guess your old Scott now—I can't keep up with you sometimes). Anyhow, Scott's been traveling around America with me and by himself for a while until he goes over to England later this month.

We zipped through Minneapolis to visit the megamall (Scott wanted to go there to purposely not buy anything), then we hung out around my folks' house in Winona for about a week before heading to Dayton, OH to see my sister and her family. We visited a friend from camp in Columbus, OH, and then headed south on the 22nd. We took back roads (Interstates suck) through KY and stayed at the Twin Knobs Recreation Area of the Daniel Boone National

Forest. It was sweet! Nice facilities—you'd like Twin Knobs (Ha!).

From there we headed south to TN. The scenes of KY and TN are beautiful. Big horse pastures, tobacco sheds—black board sheds with the ripe yellow tobacco plants curing in the heat (and humidity) of the late summer days. We decided to cruise west on Interstate 40 to see the MLK and National Civil Rights Museum in Memphis. I had Scott snap a photo of you and me (my MO tattoo) in the reflection of a picture of Rosa Parks in the museum. I hope it turns out good.

From TN we rolled south into Mississippi and camped near Sardis Lake—also very beautiful. I liked Mississippi. We found a scorpion crawling through the cold ashes of an old campfire. I had no idea they were east of the Mississippi!

We then hopped back on the Interstate and made our way south through MS to Jackson and then west on I20 to Vicksburg. We visited and toured the Civil War Memorial Park and Battlefield Site there (free admission because it was some sort of anniversary). It was awesome! To see the actual trenches and cannons, the lines of war and memorial statues and monuments—intense. We spent the afternoon there and then rolled down part of the Natchez-Trace Parkway. If you ever get a chance to travel the N.T., do it. Beauty beyond words (to my eyes anyway). Along the way, through the bayou and old plantation sites, we saw Emerald Mound near

Natchez, the second largest Indian mound in the USA. Very impressive.

We made our way to Baton Rouge, LA by about sundown. We got a Motel 6 room (what the hell, might as well) and spent the night in comfort. My car at the time was acting up a bit so we weren't sure if we should go straight on through to El Paso or travel more backcountry roads. Well, we'd both been to New Orleans already, but it's so damn cool we figured we'd take on N.O. again —and we did— Hell Yes!

I love New Awlins. We parked off of Canal St. and cruised down to Bourbon St. and the French Quarter (Preservation Hall!) and the Market Place. We just strolled around—even though (I guess) it is sort of the "off season" this time of year, it was still a good time. We had a few beers at some of the old Bourbon St. pubs and lunched on some of that great N.O. food. I found the House of Blues (my one true desire) and (contributing to their, yes, overt commercialism—but for good cause) bought a t-shirt: "On a Mission From God." Such a cool town! Architecturally, musically, soulfully, edibly, and historically—all o' that baby! We rolled out in late afternoon and made it all the way through Lafayette to Lake Charles, LA for the night.

From there we got on through half of (the widest fuckin' part of) TX to Junction (just past San Antonio by about an hour) to South Llano River State Park. There was a lot of wildlife at this park—very cool.

Deer, turkey, armadillo, raccoons. It was a full moon, river swimmin', grand old Texas night.

From there we made it to El Paso on the 28th and have been chilling out here ever since. My friend Christy lives here now, and she's got a nice place—it has been fun visiting, relaxing. Quite a road trip so far, huh? From here we plan on going up through N.M. to Flagstaff where Jessie (my old roomie in Tucson) now lives, and then up to the Grand Canyon before going back to Tucson. Then again, we may go directly to Tucson so I can find a place to live and get my car looked at.

So, what's new with you? Is your personal life steadying out? I am looking forward to seeing you again. Are you still writing? Are you still at Tribeans? Any new promotions?

I want to talk to you—I have a feeling I need to meet you face-to-face soon, like it would lead me to some higher level of insight—I still miss those spontaneous sessions at the Eagle's Nest—and our trip to Phoenix. Christopher Creek! I felt so inspired then. Inspire me, damn it! Yes, my friend, you are an inspiration—a spirit of learning and living (don't get all cocky now or anything—ha!), but know that you have a positive effect. Would you consider visiting Tucson this winter? We could go up into the mountains (really, real mountains) and chill. I would enjoy that, as I'm sure you would as well.

Well, take care, my friend. Find time to (for) yourself. Cultivate your soul. (No mud, no lotus!)

Peace, Brother.

I'll leave you with this:

> To have less
> No more
> Only essentials for warmth, education,
> shelter, exercise, music
> To travel lightly
> With everything, moving freer
> Living softer
> Loving harder, learning
> That more can be—is—less
> Less is more
> Possessions value not a person
> Judge she or he for who they are
> Not what they have
> If they have—mistakenly judge not
> What they have for who they are.
> See through to truth.
> Be open, mindful, receptive to difference.
> Differences make us common
> We all have them
> Keeping life alive

Corny or not, there it is. Keep the faith and keep your imagination fresh—it deepens that soul.

I'll write again soon with my new address as soon as I find a new home.

Later Amigo,
JT.

43.
Marc,

I want to write because I feel a need to express myself. I want to write to you because I feel I can trust you and because I feel I can say anything, even nothing, and you'll understand. I believe that may be the sign of a real, true friendship.

It is a bright, warm and sunny Tucson Sunday afternoon. The apartment is quiet, but I'll probably put some music on soon. How about Indigo Girls in your honor (12:00 Curfew?). I miss you. We should write more again. It was good to feel I could get things off my chest and get a response every week or two. Besides, I need (want) to keep writing. I keep (occasionally) thinking I would be happy getting a degree in English or even English as a Second Language (even though it's my first—and at this time only—language). I would like to learn Spanish.

I feel lost. I know the group home thing isn't something I want to do for a long time. It isn't the job so much—I think I could get good advancement with this agency—move into a more "responsible" position, more of a leadership role. But I don't know. The "system" is what sucks—the bureaucracy, the politics that are involved would sure drag a person down. It drags these kids down.

What are you doing? Are you happy? I sure wish I'll go to the mailbox and find a letter from you—any day I suppose. I know I took a long time to write back when I was at summer camp so I understand you're busy.

I just found a John Denver music book at the used bookstore so I bought it. The problem is I can only remember a couple songs, although obviously I'd know more if I heard them again. Could you suggest a collection of JD? Or maybe I can find a used copy of his greatest hits in a used CD store. Still, I will be able to play some songs soon.

I haven't smoked a cigarette in a while. I've had three in the last three weeks, all in one day. Also, (surprise) I haven't had any meat except for one lemon-peppered catfish since I got back into Tucson. It's pretty easy to be vegetarian here—lots of fruits and veggies. I eat several well-embellished homemade burritos a week—good stuff. I quit eating meat because it simply feels better—no real ethical or moral or political reason.

So can I come over and visit? Sometime around the first of November—although that is 100 percent changeable. I would like to get out and visit, maybe for a long weekend. We wouldn't have to do anything but sit and drink coffee and write and talk.

I was looking through my tapes the other day and came across one of you and me, the one we made the last time you came to visit. It sounds good, man! I can tell there's energy within it. That was a lot of fun. Have you kept up with the drums?

My traveling companion Scott and I went to visit some friends up in Flagstaff for two nights a couple weeks ago. We visited the Grand Canyon while we were there. The G.C. is awesome. Have you been there? Quite incredible!

Baked Tostitos and picante sauce is my lunch today. And a cola. I plan on going on a hike this evening—not quite sure where yet, but somewhere. I need to do <u>something</u> today.

Well, this hasn't been a very exciting letter—just babble, but I feel better. I appreciate your giving me this outlet. I still feel like I need a "creative" way to express myself. What could it be? Songwriting? I just don't know. Why write songs? I guess that's crazy. I feel good writing, but as long as it's imaginative—not just pointless babble. I think this is beginning to not make sense. I'm just going to close it, send it off, hope that you write back, and—I don't know—write about trees and birds and stuff.

But is it pointless? The mind has something to say beyond conscious thought. There's definitely something deeper underneath the voice inside my head—so profound and large that it can't fit into a voice. It must express itself through feeling. Jung might call it the Collective Unconscious. Sometimes I wonder what my point is—like now. I'll figure it out—no need to worry. It is all cyclical, right? Comes and goes—everything does. Have I told you I keep the box of your letters stuffed in my desk here at work so I can peruse/read/refer to them when I get the doldrums? Yes!

I'm including that photo I took of you, me, and Rosa Parks. It turned out pretty good, huh? You're sort of in the background, behind the OM, "quietly there" is what Scott says.

I hope to see you soon, hear from you sooner.

Peace to you, my brother.
Take care of yourself.
Jackson.

44.
Yes, JT.

I am here, and I am alive and still living in the same apartment you're mailing your letters to. Life is getting better, I guess. I've decided to just forget about my outstanding bills until which point I have some money in the bank to pay for them. That way I won't stress out so much. For some reason, thinking this way has helped a lot. Who needs good credit anyways?

My main focus right now is how to go about getting a car without any cash. I decided to go for a promotion at Tribeans, and I actually got it. I had to transfer to another store though which is 10 minutes away by car instead of a 10 minute walk. It's an hour bus ride and since buses don't start until 5:30-ish, it makes getting to the store by 5AM to open the doors a bit difficult. But I felt I had to take the job even though it's not much more money—it's a step away from Assistant Manager (which I'm striving for in about 3 months).

I've been going to a gym for about a month now—it's filled with queers (so it's okay to look, you know). I'm starting to feel better—both physically and emotionally, for now. Mentally, however, I'm still going nutso because I'm again in the process of attempting to quit smoking. It will be 10 weeks tomorrow since I've directly inhaled smoke from a smoke. I started drinking again, lightly, until it led to heavily and I told my roommate—sex buddy—whatever the fuck he is now—that I was going to hit him. Didn't remember doing that! So I haven't drank again since then (about 3 weeks). Just trying to keep a little control over my life.

I have a cold now and zits keep escaping the skin of my face. I guess perhaps the toxins from the alcohol and the cigarettes are leaving my body. That's what Norma says anyway—she's my acupuncture doctor. She's the best. I just started going to her with money I don't have. The needles provoke a feeling I've never had before—they make the qi (chi) inside my body move all around, I guess. After the acupuncture, Norma "cups" you—she puts these suction cups on your back (which leave huge hickey marks). They're supposed to suck the toxins and the stress out. There was, for sure, one knot in my back that has disappeared thanks to that process. They say acupuncture helps with emotional stuff too—it's sort of all-around healing.

I'm at work writing this right now. I got here way early since I was able to get a ride and save the buck-fifty bus fare. It's the first night I close by myself (as shift lead). Big responsibility they say. I agree—I'm kind of nervous. We just started celebrating Tribeans' 5th anniversary. It's kind of fun—we get to wear black shirts (well, dark roast coffee color) and listen to Joni Mitchell, Grateful Dead, Dylan, etc.

It's a couple days later, and I need to get this out, but I wanted to tell you of my newest inspiration. (It's amazing how just a seed of possibility can change a prolonged depressive state into a glorious week. Hope is a great thing!)

Anyhow, my district manager was talking to my manager about the developing Phoenix, Tucson, Flagstaff markets, and my name came up. I told my manager long ago, that I'd love to move to Flagstaff and manage a store out there. Turns out this spring there's going to be a big push to develop stores in AZ. Sooo, I'm going to do it! Not sure where I'll end up at first, but the goal is ultimately Flagstaff.

I'm going to get this off now. Think good thoughts...

Miss you.
Marc

45.
Marco:

INSPIRATION!! Yes! I am so glad to hear that you've again got some true spine-chilling inspiration to aim for, save for, and live for. I really, honestly, think you'd very much enjoy it in Flag. I know I would. The main reason why I don't move up there is (fear!) because I don't know if there are any real good jobs for me there. Here in Tucson, I'm working as a Behavioral Health Tech. and learning a lot. But I already know I don't want to be a social worker.

Hell man, I really have no good reason NOT to move there. Jessie and a couple other friends already live up there. To be completely honest, it is something I would work for over the winter, maybe line myself up with a job and a place to live so that by the time NAU gets out, I could move up there and probably spend what could be the best summer (and on...) of my life. I would absolutely love to live there. Options! Options! Options! I just don't know.

It sounds like you're moving into a better position with Tribeans. Pretty soon you're going to get yourself out of the big border city and up to the fuckin' mountains!! Here's a pipe dream for ya: I could move up to Flag, get a decent job, find some other cats who play guitar and start a band, start gigging around, make some extra cash while writing songs and making music! Sounds awfully appealing! Maybe if I put just a little energy into it, I could get some positive results. I bet I could damn it. Time will tell.

I went to Bookman's today and picked up an "Authentic Bluegrass Guitar" book—so, hopefully I will be able to develop some sort of skill (at least knowledge) about how to play Bluegrass (if not only my guitar better). So I'm jazzed about that. I also picked up *One Hundred Years of Solitude* by Gabriel Garcia Marquez. It is supposed to very good. I'm looking for some sort of "influence" now. I hope it will help me on my way.

I hope everything is going well for you, my friend. I want to get out to your place, but I need to find out if you'll still have a place first. Write back and let me know.

I miss you man. We need (I need) to spend some time together.

Peace to you, from me.
Jackson

46.
JT,

Yes, I am inspired. Greatly. Just having something to look forward to—i.e. getting out of this fucking state—is giving me more peace of mind than I've had in a long, long while. I think Flagstaff would be one hell-of-a-time! I think just looking up at the highest point in AZ and being around an inspiring friend would be enough to get my writing career going again. I remember I was on my way in La Crosse—holding poetry readings, writing, producing (almost) plays, etc... But being in San Diego seems to have halted all that.

Yet now some new hope is on the horizon in the form of Arizona mountains, my buddy Jackson, and some good music. And along with your band, perhaps we could work on a book, my friend. I believe we can do it.

I have no idea when Stephanie will open a Tribeans in Flagstaff, but I'm shooting to go through manager training in January. My manager says that the San Diego region might not want to spend the money training me if I'm just planning to move out of state.

Whatever.

I'm just hoping there will be a store for me by June in Flagstaff—just the word gives me tingles. They've got all the conveniences of Eastern Medicine as we do here—and natural food stores, and hiking trails, and biking trails, and mountains and skiing, and...oh my God...no way...clean air!! More chills. Does NAU have any good graduate programs? Boy, I'll probably look really old in college now.

I just went through hell last week. My roommate Gabriel disappeared for 5 days. He had my rent money—cash—which he was supposed to give to the landlord. So obviously I assumed we were going to get evicted. Gabriel finally showed up and said he spent all my money (including $2000 more that he got from maxing out his credit cards and selling the goods) to get his friend and her son off the streets of LA. He says he was embarrassed about spending my money.

He didn't even return any of my pages—just let me think that he was dead—until I finally found his sister's phone number and discovered that he had been in and out of her house the whole time. Then I was pissed! So he finally comes back, tells me the story, and borrows a thousand dollars from a friend in order to pay the rent. The landlord was cool and said he'd let us just move out at the end of the month without any penalty for breaking the lease which, might I add, is a huge relief because I can't afford this damn place on my own - $775/month!

But now I'll be able to share a cheaper place with someone else and start paying about $250 per month just in time to get my 50 cent raise from Tribeans. I may even be able to afford a junky car soon (when I move out of state of course cuz insurance is too expensive in California with smog and registration fees and shit). Shit, like I'd ever want a car here! Listen to my potty mouth!

I started smoking again after 3 months—what with all the shit that went on last week? Oh well, I've quit about 18 times. I suppose I can just quit again when I'm ready. My friend Eric says to try not counting the days next time, cuz when you count, it means you expect to do it again some day. There's some truth in that, I guess.

I just picked up, from one of the old used bookstores in town, *Yoga, Youth and Reincarnation* by Jess Stearn so I can learn some Yoga, practice some focus, and stay looking young even though I smoke. I also got a book of poems by Sylvia Plath for a little more writing inspiration. And Eric lent me his copy of *The Tenth Insight* by non other than the man himself, James Redfield. (By the way, what do you think about getting going on publishing that book? James Redfield = Spiritual inspiration; JT and Marc = inspiration for—or based on—true-life experience and feeding the soul with nature and good friendship.)

Have you read Redfield's sequel? I've only finished chapter 2. I just turned off the good ole Jayhawks and popped in some live (semi-live) Indigo Girls— who else?

I have an acupuncture appointment tomorrow—I try to fit one in whenever I have a little extra cash (paycheck tomorrow). It's much needed after all the "stress" I've been through with Gabriel. But hey, hardship = learning and knowledge. It's a necessity, right? No mud, no lotus!

Speaking of lotus, I saw Lana the other day. She's working at that bar in North Park where we used to watch the Packers games. Holy shit, that place went from a slow, neighborhood bar to a San Diego hotspot since she's started working there. She's gotta be making buck! But she still doesn't have any of that rent money she owes me. I guess I should just write that off, eh, rather than keep thinking about it and getting frustrated all the time.

Well, I guess I'll let you go now, like I've had you tied up or something—there's no rope in this letter. Or like I've nursed you back to health and am releasing you to the wild again… Hmm. This is what you're letters do for me.

Keep writing, my friend.
Marc.

47.

Marcorooni—

I got your letter today. Newz—I probably won't be able to make it over to SD before you move, but the good part is if you are going to be in Phoenix, I can visit you on weekends (yes, plural). So I hope we can start getting together and hanging out more often over the winter.

I have included the lyrics to two songs I have written. The music, of course, adds a whole different dimension to a song, but I wanted to share the words with you now—you'll hear them with music soon enough, I hope.

Road Sweat was inspired by my trip across country with Scott a couple months ago. Buddha-Man was conceived (conceptually) while listening to a tape of Jack Kerouac reciting his own poetry (yes, you can listen to it soon). I like the words and esp. the music to both of these songs. My guitar playing is improving steadily, I'm glad to say.

I have to head off to a shift of work. My hours may be (should be) changing soon to more normalized hours—1st shift Monday, Tuesday and Friday—2nd shift Wednesday and Thursday—so I would be getting Friday nights and Sat. and Sun. off. Yippie!

Mas despues.
Paz.

Ahh, off work and on to thoughts of togetherness causing inspiration leading to great jams of words and beat lines of music and poetry. I can envision right now a coffee-café in Flag.—Jack and Marc—duet poetic combo—blues and views of life, Zen and the mechanics of love. Widely divided and close-knit topics of conversation to a single drum beat and guitar strumming discordant sounds making music to our ears and money (?) from the masses. Two rucksack wanderers travelling down that four lane highway of inspiration to a beat solid and flexible with voices course but strong in soul and deep in emotion. Work on that drum man—work!

Our man Jack—Bodhisattva to jazz poets of the soul—is our godfather. Mine anyway. Listening to him recite his verse with jazz piano (Steve Allen? Really?) behind him is most excellent—even without the piano—his verse is musical in tempo and sound.

We could do it man—you with your bald-headed beret and goatee and my longer hair strapped over guitar, dressed in black, cigarettes killing us slowly, but incense burning our minds for improvisation practiced over running water at Oak Creek by Sedona. Harmonica blowing, tambourine ringing. The Shit Brother!!

I can see it now. I want you to move to Phoenix soon—ASAP—and bring that drum, your mind ready to take the next step and some beer, of course. We could really jam. I've got about 10 or so original songs right now, and I am absolutely positive that we could inspire each other to write more and more and more.

All these opportunities to pursue music and writing…

And then… The Career…

What career—my Field—what about it? I say to myself. What if I died trying to write and share my visions of Truth, Love, and Compassion in musical or poetic form—and died broke but satisfied. Or I could die having gone to school and taken the career track to social acceptance and having kept up with the Joneses for my middle and old ages.

Fuck that, man.

I want to read and write, and write and write, and play music and make a living somehow in the process…?

Now I must ask—do I actually have any talent? I think I do. I'm not "gifted"—I need to work at my abilities, but we all have to work at some things, don't we? My passion is in words and music. Why not follow that dream, pursue that bliss?

I don't know my brother. I'm sitting here on a Friday night drinking beer and writing you a letter and on occasion picking up my guitar, working on my technique, emotion, soul, and vocal qualities, writing and singing to you my friend. Here is a

185

poem I wrote on the way to work today (started in my car and finished in the parking lot).

When you're in
Love
When you're out
Of love
Know that knowing not
Is the key
Of surrender to nothingness
Into fear
Allow entrance
Of self
Allow revelry in depth
Into kindness
Respect individuality
In others
Respect oneness
Of humanity
Allow expectation to drop
Like rain drops
Into a lake
Jumping in love
Getting wet all over

I'm not sure about the last two lines yet—or the whole thing for that matter. You're the educated English one. You can tell if it's any "good." All I can tell is that it is of feeling from inside and has been expressed into this current form. You know literature and form and content. Where am I among the literati and experienced? Among the educated and learned? Should I care? In many ways I don't because what I write is of and for myself.

Whatever... as you and Ted say.

Soon (I so hope) we could be sharing some beers and kicking back constructing phrases and ideas from each other's minds. Now that would be dreamy!

I've started reading *Way of the Peaceful Warrior* by Dan Millman. I know you had read and recommended it quite a while ago. One passage, or sentence anyway, I've found has been: "When you lose your mind, you come closer to your senses" (Millman 75). Dig it. I believe I need to start losing my mind again (like I did when I got my MO tat).

I am currently sitting at Bentley's House of Coffee and Tea, sipping a cranberry herbal tea (strong!). I have brought some paper and writing utensils (although I could have done better than two unsharpened number 2 pencils and a medium point Papermate pen that farts turds on every few words—but I'm not complaining). Also I have a few dollars for some tea as well as some Fig Newtons hidden in my knapsack. I also have your last letter.

The music here is feedback drenched rock-n-roll, maybe Velvet Underground. I've also got some books—Millman, plus *One Hundred Years of Solitude* as well as a Cornell West bestseller *Race Matters*, in case different cravings (for knowledge) would strike me.

I want a pair of big black engineer boots, "In my big black boots" I'll stomp and romp all across this land.

Bob Dylan is <u>still the man</u>!!

I am SO excited for your move to AZ. I hope everything works out for you. For those in search or pursuit of their dream, The Way will guide you, if you open up to it. And I believe you are. I can't wait.

Humanity is so diverse, isn't it? Why can't we all just get along?!?! How can some people look so beautiful until they open their mouths and let all kinds of ignorance spill out. I guess that is an outer beauty without the inner companion, or compassion.

This woman I've been seeing, Julie, is definitely a beauty inside and out. She is actually quite pretty but even more beautiful inside. A big heart and passion. I want you two to meet. I think you'd like each other, spiritually.

Well, I think I have possibly rambled on enough for one sitting. I hope you will let me know soon what your plans for the not-too-distant future will be.

I do wish I could make it out to SD to see you once more (and who knows—it might happen), but I am anxiously awaiting word about your impending move to Phoenix. How excellent that would be!!

If I were to move to Flag., could you hook me up with a job at Tribeans? How is it working for a corporate giant? What is the opening pay? Benefits? (besides all the coffee).

Take care of yourself. Cut the smokes. I hope you enjoy the songs (lyrics).

Peace, love and music,
Jackson.

ROAD SWEAT

Road Sweat, don't come off easy
Road Sweat, you know I feel greasy
Road Sweat, dripping down my spine,
getting in my eyes

Funky as the road can be
Just outside Nashville, Tennessee
Jump in the river, wash yourself clean
You're leavin' sweat stains on my seat!

Chicago to Tuscaloosa; New Orleans to El
Paso
We don't need no stinkin' showers—hit the
road with no hassle.

Road Sweat, Road Sweat
Marking off the miles
When I'm sweaty, nobody smiles

Stay off the Interstate
It's all that traffic I hate
Roll down the window, so I can see and
hear the wind blow
Through my harp I play vibrato!

Kentucky to Vicksburg, Mississippi to the
Delta
When you're sweatin' on the highway, no
one pulls over to help ya

Sun goin' down I can barely see
What's that sign up in front of me?
Pull over to the side of the road, so I can see
What's that, they got air-conditioning?

Road Sweat, don't come off easy. Road
Sweat you know I feel greasy. Road Sweat
dripping down my spine, but you know I
feel fine when I'm on… On the Road. On the
Road. On the Road…

YOU ARE NOT MY BUDDHA-MAN

You are not my Buddha-Man, watching my
every move
You are not my Buddha-Man, tripping up
my groove
In the mail, on the highway, you think
you've got control
Of me, my mind, and my way, but you're
moving a bit too slow

Buddha-Man, Uncle Sam
I don't look up to you
Buddha-Man, Charlie Chan
Your image I see right through

You are not my Buddha-Man controlling all
the masses
You are not my Buddha-Man, congress of
fat asses
You don't compensate the exploited folk,
affirm diversity
You got no pride, no self-respect, no well-
built dignity

CHORUS—inst. bridge—Solo

Now the one and only true Buddha-Man
comes out of the East
You are not my Buddha-Man, with you I
will not feast
On pork roasted slowly over slavery and the
theft
Of lands and minds and bodies, without
them what is left?

CHORUS—inst. bridge—Solo—End.

48.
Hello Jackson!

Good to see you've been loaded with creativity and
have been getting it onto paper. I'm sure your songs
all sound cool to music, but the one I like best—just
having seen the words—is "You Are Not My
Buddha-Man." Keep writing originals, JT—you are
on your way.

And yes, I think it is very important (yes, I said "important") to follow your dreams. However, I've discovered/decided that it's a lot less stressful (although <u>rewarding</u> I have not yet thought about) to be financially secure first. Now that I think about the rewarding part, the <u>feeling</u> of being rewarded would probably be greater if there was a lot of struggle getting there—I mean struggle in all aspects of life—that may give someone more to write about too. As for myself, my financial stress—bills and all—just got to be too much to handle so I decided I had to do something about it—and I think I'm getting there.

I am sooo looking forward to sitting around drinking a beer with you and writing songs and poetry and other creative endeavors like stories and <u>our book</u>—ooo, I just got a little chill—that's a good thing.

Hey, it sounds like your little change in hours is going to be pretty damn awesome. You'll have a somewhat normal 9-5 sort of job.

I might have to get a car when I move there unless I can find a cheap studio apartment very close to my store. Maybe we could take a ski trip too, somewhere to the north—it's been about two years since I've been skiing—way too long. You know what, in a month and a half, I will have been in San Diego an entire year—wow—and I'm getting giggly about getting to leave soon.

Man, I'm rereading your letter and am again amazed at how you have a way with words, such as: "Jack and Marc—duet poetic combo—blues and views of life, Zen and the mechanics of love. Widely divided and close-knit topics of conversation to a single drum beat and guitar strumming discordant sounds making music to our ears and money (?) from the masses." Etc. Etc. It goes on obviously, but I'm not going to write your entire letter back to you—so poetically energized and stimulating! I put your letter down and sigh… My roommate gazes at me with a questioning look. I say, "This is what inspires me."

"What, letters from him?" asks Bobby (by the way, I'm staying with Bobby again in his tiny studio apt. for the meantime).

"Yes," I say. "The way he writes, his views, his dreams, and knowing I have a friend out there who can influence me and help guide me toward my own dreams."

JT, you don't know how much your friendship means to me. You've got to understand that you are my rock. Every time I receive a letter from you, I again feel grounded in my life, and balance is something I need right now in order to achieve and live out my dreams. Thank you!

I'm sitting at my old store (in Hillcrest) overhearing a priest and another guy talking about the proposition in CA that passed to allow medical use of marijuana when recommended by a physician.

193

They seem quite upset, "appalled" I just heard. I don't know much about the proposition so I can't make an opinion right now. Maybe we can chat about it sometime soon.

Yes, I'm almost positive I could get you a job at Tribeans in Flagstaff. Stephanie has said that her "intuition" is telling her that there will be at least a couple of stores in Flagstaff. This is just a thought: if you got a part time job at a Tribeans in Tucson, then you could end up being a lead or even an assistant manager in Flagstaff... Like I said, just a thought.

Well, I'm going to send this off now—I will keep in touch soon to let you know the news about my move.

Keep writing JT. I'm trying to cut down on the smokes.

Take care,
Marc!

49.
JT,

The middle of January is when I will send up the sail and catch the eastbound breeze to a new land. Phoenix or Tucson, wherever my DM wants/needs me. Probably Phoenix. I'm just going to stay at my store here through Christmas and a couple weeks after to catch a lot of the returns/exchanges. I'll find out where I'm actually going in a couple of weeks.

I just went today to see if I could get a car loan. I'm praying—I am completely sick of not having transportation! Besides, my new DM in SD told my manager that I have to get a car to have totally open availability or think about stepping back down to barista. The only hours I can't really make it to work right now are 5-7 in the morning because the buses don't run that early. What ticks me off is that one of our other leads has a completely tighter availability—a few hours on one day—from 5-1 the next—and on and on. Oh well, I guess it's something I have to deal with, but this seniority, pal-to-pal, good ol' boy shit has never thrilled me.

Speaking of cars, how's the Caprice running? I have to say you made quite a great buy with that beast. WI to AZ to WI and back? Hell, why didn't you just drive to the moon? Gosh, I'm so creative. Ha!

Perhaps it's a reason why I've been so dry recently in my writing. The feeling of being stuck in one place—without a car or a lot of money—can create a slight form of depression. Lately I've noticed myself thinking that I just want to get out and go somewhere else—I know this seems like a common theme with me—but here I mean even somewhere else in San Diego—like to the gym—just <u>anywhere</u> to get away. But I can't because of the bus schedule making things tight with my work schedule or there being no public bus headed to my destination.

When I feel this way, I get depressed or upset and end up doing nothing but lying around. I know I should take advantage of the time I'm stuck at home and write or something, but I often feel empty and void (within) which would resonate in my writing. I don't want my writing to feel empty (maybe it would be kind of neat—I don't know—there was something sort of "empty" within the pages of that Sylvia Plath book).

Hmm. Why don't I just wait a couple days and see what happens. I feel like I need to write my dad and say hi.

Take care Bud!
Keep in touch!
Marc

50.
Jackson,

How are you Bud? I guess, along with this letter, which I hope will bring you a few smiles, I will also toss to you many holiday bells of cheer. I hope you will have someone to spend the holidays with. I was worried about that for a long time cuz I usually seem to get mushy (somewhat) around Christmas time, but just yesterday I got a call from my friend Kevin from Milwaukee (I worked with him at McDonald's for two years in high school and then initially went to college with him in La Crosse until he transferred).

Anyhow, he's finally moving out here. He left yesterday, so I'm expecting him tomorrow or Saturday. He and his friend are going to stay here for a couple days until they find a place to live. It's a good thing my roommate is going to LA—to his mom's—for 5 days during the holidays—cuz our apt. is so tiny. Kevin was supposed to move out here in August, but he's put it off this long—I guess he knew I needed a nice Christmas gift!

Have I told you this yet? I had to buy a car—so I did. Stepping down to barista wasn't an option for me so I went to a couple car dealerships and finally found one who would finance me for a little tiny 1994 Geo Metro. It kicks ass man. It's blue and has the fully decked out AM/FM radio with front speakers! It does have AC though which I made sure of since I'm moving to Phoenix soon.

Update: I don't know when yet.

Yes, that's my update. My manager and I have been doing a lot of "off-the-floor training" in the past couple weeks which I'm completely grateful for. She told me she doesn't want me waiting around for an Assistant Manager position once I get there. She wants to be able to say, with pride, that I'm ready.

How are your new hours working out? How's the relationship going? Basically, how's life been treatin' ya? Hope to hear from you soon. It's been a while… Gabriel won't call me back ever and still owes me $400 for the phone bill—oh well, that's another dilemma.

See you soon JT!
Love ya! And happy holidays!
Marc.

51.
Dear Jackson,

Did you move? Get evicted? Are you alive? Gotten my letters? I suppose you're just busy, but I needed to write again since I have another...

UPDATE: Tribeans SUCKS! How is it working for a corporate giant, you ask? Fucking sucks! You can't even be human—you have to be a fucking machine!

So, I'm grinding beans and I'm tapping the side of the grinder so the beans empty. There's nothing worse than having a clump of old ground beans fall into a fresh bag of coffee, nor is it appropriate to hand someone a pound of beans they paid good money for (an outrageous amount of money actually) but which only has .91 of a pound it in cuz the rest is stuck in the grinder.

Anyways, in front of the customer, the district maintenance guy YELLS at me! I'm the supervisor on duty and this guy fucking yells at me in front of the customer! So I try to make a joke of it so it seems like, to this customer anyway, like he was just joking. And then the guy YELLS at me more!

So I sort of roll my eyes to the customer, give her the coffee, and wish her a good day, and then try to talk with the guy. Who knew the maintenance guys ran everything?! Anyhow, I almost lost it on him in front of my manager and Stephanie (the DM—yes, she had to be there). I tried to get my mgr. to admit that this guy has been a chronic asshole (which he has

198

been and she knows it), but she says, get this, "I don't know what you're talking about, Marc."

What?! Either she's fucking the guy or it's the climbing the corporate ladder bullshit that I fleetingly thought would be good for me...

So, I walked out.

It's got to be money-strapped passion for me, rather than financially secure BULLSHIT! And what the fuck, perhaps I won't be broke forever...

I've got an idea for a book already. It's an examination of human sexuality. It occurred to me that you just might be a bit gay. Now, don't get upset and try to huff and puff in order to prove you're not (like too many folks do). That's not the point I'm making. In fact, you're probably less gay than most people in the world. My concept, if true—and using my logic, I'm thinking it's got to be true—would be great for everyone in the world, not just LGBT folks. It would even be good for the liberation of the male, for I'm sure you've wanted to hug me before without people thinking you're a homo (although now that you've gone and tattooed my initials on your bod, makes me think that maybe you actually ARE in love with me). To tell you the truth, I believe you truly are a hetero, but I also know you wanted to hug me at the airport in Phoenix when we first said goodbye, and I felt the hesitation from every cell in your body... And I understand. This macho world we live in will soon melt, especially if we all come to a new understanding of human sexuality.

Hear my out. I believe that sexual preference lies on a bell curve. Most people are of "average" sexual preference (just like most people are of "average" intelligence or "average" height. But, obviously in this world, when given the ability to choose a mate, the people who have the ability to LOVE someone of the opposite sex (even if they have the <u>ability</u> to LOVE either sex) will CHOOSE to love the opposite sex because living a homosexual lifestyle in today's society is a bit challenging, to say the least!

So, think of how understanding this would change the world. Assumptions would be shattered and belief systems would go haywire. Some lives or families would probably even be torn apart in the short run. Yet far more lives will be liberated and invigorated in the short run and for sure in the long run. In fact, whole worlds will open up, possibilities will be endless, understanding of one-another will create peace, children will grow up more happily, more marriages will be seen through, the population will stabilize, bullying will wane, and ultimately lives will be saved.

It will be called *The Gay Bell Curve*, by Marcus Ortega. When I remember back over my life, I realize this concept has got to be true. I know tons of my neighbors and friends and my brother's friends had messed around. They were tight, enjoyed each other's company immensely, and messed around sexually, I know. I know! But now so many of them are married with children... They can't <u>all</u> be unhappily married gay guys, you know?

One of the main arguments that gay rights advocates and most out gay individuals try to force down other people's throats is that being gay is not a choice. Well, I think this is an argument that will <u>never</u> be won by either party. First off, why would anyone in this society of violence and bigotry toward gays ever make the <u>choice</u> to live a gay lifestyle? It just doesn't make sense, right?

But we can look at this argument from the other side too. How could anyone even think that homosexuality is a choice unless <u>they themselves</u> have made that choice? So, in essence, bisexuals who have made the choice to live a straight lifestyle (and this is the majority of the people in the world according to a traditional bell curve) MUST be the ones making and attempting to defend this argument that homosexuality is a choice. When I considered this possibility, everything began to fall into place and finally make sense.

Here's an example: After a few years of living "out," my father asked me to try living straight for a while, since I'd already given the gay lifestyle a shot (like I hadn't tried that already). This comment begs the question of whether he's had homosexual feelings or experiences. I remember him getting all giddy when an old friend of his from high school came to the house for a visit. He wanted to hold the door for him, to walk him to his car, and he smiled like I'd never seen him smile before... And when you really think about it, even suggesting the notion of trying out a certain sexual preference leads me to the conclusion that the person making the suggestion has thought about trying it—if he were completely straight, he wouldn't even think there would be the possibility of switching teams.

Here's another memory: Upon coming out to a coworker when I was working at Fat Sam's Burgers in La Crosse, one question he had for me was: what could I find in a guy that I couldn't find in a girl? I really couldn't answer that question at the time, aside from the obvious: a penis. Pondering this a while though, I've come to wonder what exactly he meant. He must have found that he could develop feelings of love and attraction for both men and women. He must have had bisexual feelings, though he chose to live a heterosexual lifestyle.

My mom, too (along with most mega-religious peeps, I'd imagine), really believes that God is testing me by putting this "temptation" into my heart. This tells me that she and others in the church have been tempted with the sexually "deviant" beast of homosexuality (or adultery for that matter— though I'm not sure how the bell curve would apply to that).

I guess the church is GENIUS in this as well—you need God to overcome your temptation to stray toward the deviant, right? Please. My mom continues to think I'm an immoral person, but I just can't seem to understand how being honest and true to a lover (ie. being in love with another guy, or even saying, "sorry _female_ I can't marry you because I'm actually <u>gay</u>") could possibly be more immoral than actually going through with something I know isn't right and would be <u>completely unfair</u> to any wife or any children that may be produced as a result.

Here's the real deal now: the majority of people have these feelings of being able to love whomever they <u>choose</u> because most people (about 65%) lie somewhere in the middle of the bell curve. As an example, Intelligence has most often been plotted on an IQ scale with 100 being of average intelligence. 65% of people fall into the 85-115 IQ range, 15% fall into the 60-84 range, 15% fall into the 116-140 range, and 5% fall above 140 or below 60, creating a bell curve when plotted on a graph. Height is the same way and, when plotted, also creates a bell curve. If you apply this to sexual preference, then about 65% of all people are between about 40-60% gay (amazing, huh).

Currently, many people who are mostly gay are encouraged (forced?) through society's norms to marry, have a family, and try to deny or "repent" and squash the natural feelings they are having and have had all their lives. The unintended consequences of denying your true or natural self may include self-hatred, substance abuse, depression, suicide, child abuse, or even homicide. Gosh, this comes up over and over again, doesn't it—this cyclical stuff we're never going to overcome in our current religion-based and competition-based society.

Wow, this letter is getting long and babbly, but since you haven't been writing, I guess I'll make up for your lack of it.

Hey, sorry I'm not going to be moving out there. Maybe it's for a reason. Who knows, maybe we'd end up hating each other. All things are for the best, don't you think?

I gotta tell you, I'm not all that broken up about Tribeans—look at the inspiration I've found... I feel like I'm back on my creative path rather than beating my head against the corporate concrete ceiling.

My friend Kevin got stuck in Missouri and decided to go back home—engine troubles (old camper-van)—but still I'm feeling good man! I'm feeling free and fresh. Get back to me, Jackson. I miss ya!

Peace and good bluegrass music.
Marc

52.
Jack,

Not sure what I've done, if I said something, if I sent some sort of off-energy, or just got too negative at times. But whatever it is, I apologize. I am just being Me, that which I thought I could be, whenever I hung with/wrote to you. I am hoping there is an explanation, though I'm not sure what it could be other than just a simple case of "you take too much energy to maintain our friendship." I know how it is. I've had friends in the past who were that way. But I thought we were different.

I've told you stories of growing up, of questioning everyone and everything. And I know it gets cumbersome sometimes, but I am learning/trying to stay upbeat. I have tried to be who others see/want me to be, but as you know, that's no good for the soul, for the long term, for the eternal.

That's what I don't get. We are ALL one. You and me and the trees and the insects, and even all those I despise for bringing me down (like the Madre) and forcing me to live within the boundaries of my fear, fear that they've engrained in me (although I guess they don't <u>know</u> they're doing it). But even they and we are ONE. Can't we just get through this together?

My friend, Jackson, you are like none other. Please don't let this awesome thing we've got fall apart.

For now, I will think good thoughts, for the great masters know that they are things (thoughts) and you will receive them through the ether...

Please write, bud.
Marc

53.
Jack Jackson,

My mother hates sin. She tells me so. She loves me, of course—she says that too, but she just can't allow me to be around her and her family because she hates sin so much. So I can't see my little brother (who is 9 now) because she's afraid I "might give him something." Yes, she said that right to my face—well, over the phone.

Oh, where the fuck are you when I need you!

I was talking to a friend here, a spiritual woman named Christy who is shown flowing images of the energy potentials of the future. She says some of the feelings—or "images"—she gets are stronger than others because they are more likely based on the current emotions/emotional states or energy matrices that are created everyday by all of our (human beings') thoughts. Each time we think a thought, the energy matrices change, she says, so if we stay on a thought about something we want for our future for long enough (longer than other thoughts about our future at least), then the energy matrices will begin to change to be more aligned with the things we want.

Well, I tend to believe these things, whether true or not. My attitude is that if the placebo works, use it!

So, Christy says there is a small possibility (energy matrix of potentiality) right now for me to become a leader in the creative arts, but the larger matrix she sees is that of a helper, a teacher... We'll see where that goes.

She also says that just under the helper/teacher energy matrix there is a spiraling blob of black energy. I asked her if it was evil, and she said "only if you believe in evil." Interesting. She then said that she doesn't ever see evil because it does not exist, but it's just a blob of non-intention, of non-thought, if you want to think of it that way. Like if someone just let life go by without much effort, much thought, or without really learning anything. (I think of those redneck arguments over regular or light beer that we've discussed in the past.)

So she says this potential exists there, underneath my stronger matrix (as of right now), this possibility of retreating to a life of blah, of non-thinking, of coasting, being "content" but bored, I guess.

I've got to tell you, that scares the fuck out of me. I would absolutely hate myself on my deathbed to think I've wasted so much time just drifting.

Anyway, remember how I've always wanted to go to the mountains? To live in solitude and find my creative spark? Well, in order to avoid being that drifter I so fear, and since I'm not moving to Phoenix (and you seem to no longer be around), I've decided it's time to do it. Mountains, here I come.

If you have been reading my letters, you may remember that I told you I wrote to my dad. Anyhow, all this shit has been on my mind a great deal lately, so in my letter to him, I told him of my quest to discover who I truly am and why I'm here. (He's always been so supportive—much more so than the Madre, obviously). So, he's never told me this before, but apparently my dad's uncle, I guess that would be my great uncle (I think?), is a priest in Chile. My dad said he talked to his uncle Fernando who said I could go visit San Benito de LLiu LLiu, in the V region of Chile (my homeland man!). They're building a community garden this summer (their summer—now), and he said they need plenty of help. It will be interesting getting to see how they live, maybe relearning some of my Spanish, and hopefully I will be comfortable asking lots of questions.

So, I'm going, damn it!

I've finally made my decision—whether it's the best thing for me now or not, at least it will be experience. I am seeking knowledge man. I want to learn who I am, who I really am inside. I'll learn something about myself and the world, I know it. But above all else, I won't let that black blob of potential energy that has been lurking in my matrix of potentiality gain any more strength.

In fact, maybe I'll meditate away my shroud of fear and let that blob float away altogether. That would be great. Maybe I'll even find out who the real Marcus Ortega is, for if you seek, you will find, right?

So, I really hope to hear from you, but I'm not sure I'll get your letters anytime soon even if you do write. I'll put a forward on my mail and send you my new address in Chile when I find out what it is—if I'll even be allowed (or able) to receive mail.

So, my friend—and I hope I can still call you my friend—until we meet again…

M.O.

54.
Mr. Ortega!

How the hell are ya! Of course you can call me your friend. Always, my man. Always. Yes, there was a hiccup in my whole life and definitely my mail situation. I actually decided to do it, to move to Flagstaff and the mountains, the veggie cafes, the farmers' markets, the music and all the cool, cool cats. I put a hold on my mail before I moved up, and Jessie's house (where I was planning to stay until I was able to find a more stable apartment of my own) was suddenly filled with houseguests. The winter seems to bring up folks from Phoenix and Tucson, while Christmas vacation seems to have brought in plenty of folks from our old stomping ground—the Midwest.

Anyways, I had to hurry to find a vacant apartment (since I needed to move in ASAP). I've ended up settling for a lease and paying <u>way</u> too much in rent as a result. Then, the money fairies must have been angry (not that I believe in fairies), because the transmission finally dropped out of the Caprice. It sucks, but at least it (the transmission) waited until I was in my new environment and didn't choose to fall out on the way up (or in El Paso or New Orleans for that matter). It would have been expensive had I decided to fix it so I am currently leaning toward junking it and buying new—well, new used anyway. But I wanted to settle in and find a job first before I forked over any cash to fix or buy. I wasn't sure how long it would take me to find work. But, after only 10 weeks or so (wow, ugh), I finally found a job.

So there the mail sat, bundled up in a Tucson post office. I had been planning to drive down to retrieve it, along with my last paycheck and a few things from my desk at the boys' home (including your latest letters with your latest—at the time anyway—address), but the Chevy was busted.

Sorry, bro. I hope you can forgive me. I would have written sooner, believe me. It sounds as if I've missed quite a bit of change in your life. I hope Chile is treating you well. Again, you ARE my <u>main man</u>! You know that, right?

I'm back—it's a couple days later. So I told you I found a job, right? Anyhow, I thought maybe I would leave this part out, but I should probably let you know that the job I found (part time at least until I am able to secure something more in my field in the future) is at the brand new, opening soon, very first Flagstaff AZ Tribeans! Yes, I took your advice. Although now, finally having gotten all your letters and having read about your horror serving corporate America, I'm not so sure Tribeans is the place to be. O well, I guess I will see where it goes. Training starts next week.

I have decided to junk the Caprice. I found a new (used, slightly) truck, a 1994 Ford Ranger that I can afford payments on for at least the next 5 or 6 months (along with my rent) until things would start to get a bit tight. I hope to find full time employment by then—or maybe be making some extra dough from playing gigs of my own—we'll see.

My girlfriend Julie is planning to move up here soon too. Did I tell you about her? You <u>have</u> to meet her. She would be something like your spiritual sister. She's a practitioner of Somatic Psych, using holistic approaches to the body as self in a therapeutic setting, sort of trying to bridge the mind-body connection through examining how the mind affects the body as well as how the body (movement, stillness, meditation, sense perception, acupressure, acupuncture, etc.) affects the mind. Cool stuff. I think you'd like her. She has always wanted to try living up here in the mountains as well, so she's wrapping up some things down in Tucson, getting her house ready to sell, etc. She will be traveling back and forth for a while at first (until the house sells at least) while she's setting up her own practice up here in Flag. Hopefully it will go well for her here.

I haven't written too much lately. There is an open mic starting up at a nearby pub on Tuesday nights that I will attend and hopefully meet some other guitar guys and maybe a drummer or two, I hope. Maybe there'll be enough to put a little band together.

Well, my main señor, you take it easy (like <u>that</u> will be hard for you).

Meditate mucho!
Jack

55.
Hola Jackson.

There are hills surrounding the San Benito Monastery like those that nestled Lake Patagonia within them. They are dry and the dust settles evenly onto the open windowsills of my dormitorio. They are adding yet another addition to the east wing of the monastery—the construction sounds are welcome remembrances of some semblance of civilization. Even in my meditation, they seem as the backdrop drum beats of the new rhythm of my life. They are magical, as are the heavy accents of a language that I am still so unfamiliar with. I imagine, with time, my focus will turn from inside myself to the conversations of the workers, as my understanding of the language grows. Not sure if that's a good thing.

The grounds here are beautifully manicured and expanding every day. There are four other volunteers here right now—two leave next week back to Germany and the others (American friends from California—though quite kind, they are more body and mind oriented than here for spiritual growth) leave in about 3 months. Prior Edwards hopes to get a few more year-long volunteers from the German crop soon.

The creek north of the monastery has been a necessary outlet for sure. It gets hot, and though the breezes are dry, it's nice to take a little dip after digging up ground and pouring concrete all day.

I need you to know my news Jack! It's going to be awesome! This is probably my last letter to you.

I really hope you have a good explanation for not writing—bitch! I am not sure if I will even have much time to write—well, I will probably have plenty of time but perhaps not for writing. It will take a month for letters to get to you anyhow. Besides, I also hate to keep hounding you if you have become uninterested, but I desperately want you to know what I'm doing (and I too want to know what and how <u>you</u> are doing).

That said, I won't be receiving mail for some time so if you write (or if you have written—and perhaps you have, I hope), I will not read your letters until I return from my <u>extended retreat</u>.

I am on my way to China!

Prior Edwards here at San Benito hooked me up with a Tibetan Gompa (monastery) in Dranang—"south of the mountains." It's called Samye. It's the first ever monastery built in Tibet. Prior Edwards met a monk from there on a compassion journey (mission) to Somalia. Apparently I must have been asking too many questions here, to the point that the Prior wants to get rid of me. Prior Edwards says there is money available to "folks like you who ask a lot of questions in the search for self." (You know how I am.) All I had to do was write a "thank you" note to an anonymous donor for paying for my travel there.

So, off I go, mañana!

I'm fucking nervous as HELL! (Oops, I shouldn't be potty-mouthing here...holy place, you know.) I think Samye should be more interesting than it has been here at the LLiu LLiu. I'll get to learn some chanting, and Prior Edwards says more of the people there speak English than they do here and they have more recreations (times that it's okay to speak—yay!). I'm nervous but looking forward to it.

My meditation practice has regained some steam (or less steam, however you look at it). I've been sitting consistently for about an hour and a half each day and am ultimately shooting for 4 hours each day (two in the morning and two at night).

Prior Edwards has been nice, but I'm not sure I'm cut out for the Catholic/Judeo Christian thing. I lean East, you know. I've gained some <u>real</u> insight into my Self, but still I struggle with <u>Dios</u>. Even Prior Edwards has said to me, "You must have Faith, my son." Ughh!

Wish me luck.
Marcus

    The last of Marc's letters didn't get to Jack as quickly as either of them would have liked. I ponder this issue now, during our current era of email, Facebook, text messaging, video chatting, and all the technology that connects us so well these days. But in the spring of 1997, even cell phones were still in their infancy. In fact, fax machines and pagers were still heavily in use, which reminds me of the old 8-track jokes of my childhood.

Marc never received the latest of Jack's letters before he left on his journey, and forwarding them to Marc in Tibet never happened. Marc had requested, through the post office, that all of his mail be forwarded to his father's house, and he asked his dad to send any good mail, such as letters from friends, to him in Chile. But as a result of Marc's short stay in Chile, and his subsequent move half a world away, his father had chosen to hang on to the letters until Marc returned to the states.

Jack was surprised to find a letter in the mail addressed to him from Raymond Ortega, Marc's dad.

56.

Hello Jackson,

My name is Raymond Ortega. I am the father of Marcus. I have the letter you recently sent to Marcus here for safekeeping since he has gone searching for something of treasure to him. I know you two must be good friends as he has talked about you and I know he has traveled the country with you. Along with his belongings, which he has stored at my house while he is gone, I am also holding a stack of letters that are mostly, it appears, from you. Please know that he has saved them and he will collect them upon his return. Also, please know that upon his return, I will be showing him how proud I am of him and how much I love him, and I hope his friends will do the same. Marcus will be leaving to Tibet for an extended stay at a temple in Dranang. I have spoken to the Prior at San Benito in Chile, where Marcus has spent some time. The Prior knows his heart and has said that we must support Marcus in his journey. Please continue your friendship with my son and support him upon his return. It is very important to him.

Sincerely,
Raymond Ortega

57.
Jackson,

I am at Samye, and I've snuck off to the forest for a bit. I wish to retreat to the mountains, but they are dry and look unforgiving. The trip here was long, dusty, and wore heavily on my body, especially the final leg of the journey to Samye. I was tired, so tired, and the bus just about bounced the bones out of my skin.

But I am here, alive.

My favorite monk is a 51 year-old bald guy (they're all pretty much bald—although some need a haircut) from Wuhan China who transplanted here from the holy city of Lhasa. He blames me for trying to make him laugh during evening meditation (I swear I'm not—perhaps it's my face reacting from the pain of sitting still for two hours at a time!). His name's Duga, but I call him Dougie Fresh (that's to make him laugh). Though we tease, he's been way helpful with my meditation practice. It's crazy how different it is here. It's almost like the zeal/zest for life here is amplified, especially compared to San Benito. At SB it seemed I was trying to please all the time, or like I had to watch myself so I didn't piss anybody off. Prior Edwards was nice, don't get me wrong, but there was some sense of authority that kept me sort of fearful all the time (if I had to put an emotion to it).

Here at Samye, though, it's like I'm hovering above myself, like I'm higher (emotionally AND spiritually) than I've ever been before. I don't even feel like I CAN mess up here. All the monks smile all the time—they are able to settle in to their meditations so quickly—it's like it's a sexual experience for them.

I've noticed the younger ones stretch afterwards with huge smiles while the older ones (Dougie Fresh included) just have the simplest, most content smirks I've ever seen—like a knowledge of having just been within the spirit of the universe. I too have been <u>loving</u> my meditations, and I've been so focused and content (even though we don't do much and have to be silent much of the day—we get to read at least). It's crazy though because I don't feel like I'm actually meditating a lot of the time anymore—I feel like the first few weeks I was able to feel my body relax and see (in my mind) my flesh drip off of my spirit, but lately (even though I feel so content afterwards), I feel like my mind has been extra active during sitting.

217

I asked Duga why my mind wanders so much now, especially these last few days here. He said that as it becomes easier to quiet the mind during meditation, it too becomes easier to allow the mind to explore the universal energy source during that time—he calls it "basking in the awe of the source." Sometimes I can totally feel it. In essence, perhaps I am becoming calmer and a bit more focused, like I have been feeling, even though my mind is "exploring" more during meditation.

I remember this wandering mind of mine being the cause of my frustration with my meditation practice in the past. Duga also taught me not to judge my meditations, that judgment is a form of ego, and ego is a human trait that is not everlasting. I used to get so upset when some of my meditation sessions were basically useless (I thought) because I couldn't focus, because there was so much gunk stuck up there in the mind, that it caused me to want to quit meditating (but now I believe it is a process of growing more deeply in touch with "God" (or "the universal spirit").

It's interesting that this natural growth is often the reason that people don't stick with their meditation practice. I guess we all need meditation coaches, even though we don't often admit it. Duga's my dude! He says the God I've been searching for is actually my Self—the true essence of Me—Marcus Ortega. "M—O," he said.

Then, humorously, at the end of yesterday's meditation (we usually chant for 30 minutes then end with six "OM's"), Duga led the OM's, and on the third and fourth OM's, he actually said, "MO" and I saw him looking at me out of the corner of his eye. He wouldn't admit it after—he just said that my mind only hears what it wants to hear, then he smirked. That's Duga!

I've been learning so much here Jack—and it's only been a few weeks. There is NO focus here on anything negative—I've been corrected already when I was talking to Duga and a couple other bald guys about stopping hunger in the world, and they said that we do not talk about hunger here, we talk about prosperity and joy and having enough for everyone to eat, "all things positive." We don't surround ourselves here with news of the world because all they ever report these days is the bad stuff that's happening, and "negativity brings more negativity" is what Duga says. That, and "positivity brings positivity" and "joy brings joy." And then someone inevitably cracks a joke about there being so much joy in the world that there's not enough time to meditate on all of it so instead they'll just think about nothing. It's funny how they really don't have to explain what they mean either—I already understand, it seems, as soon as it comes out of their mouths. And they never have to "sell" their ideas. I remember with Prior Edwards, I was always asking follow-up questions, "why this, why that" because nothing seemed to "add up."

Here though, Jack, everything just makes sense to me—well, MOSTLY. I asked Duga a few days ago about his family, and he said, "This is my family.

You are my family." I told him that my mom is the best ever at guilt-trips and that she judges me all the time and tells me she only does so because she doesn't want me to go to Hell. Duga said there is no Hell—he said there are only good things—love, joy, compassion, and all things positive will last forever and that death only returns us to the one universal energy that is ALL things.

I asked him how I should deal with my mom when she judges me, and Duga said, "The secret of living with joy and compassion is to have no fear. Surround yourself with all things positive."

I asked him then that if my mom was only causing me frustration, anger, resentment, and to fear God and death (judgment day), then was I supposed to just ignore her, my own flesh and blood?

Duga responded, "Flesh and blood are not eternal. Only joy, love, compassion—all things positive."

You hear that Jackson? Flesh and blood are <u>not</u> eternal! Flesh and blood are NOT eternal!

I understood! Finally! (And you were right!)

I can't keep perpetuating the negativity, the fear, the judgment that my mother feeds me. I feel so, so good here, finally—away from the pressures of the ego-based attitudes that exist in a Christian-based society that is the US of A. Away from the desire (or the need sometimes) to do things because <u>others</u> have dreams for me, away from having to live up to expectations that others have placed on me, away from the pressures of paying the bills, the rent, phone, and heat, the credit cards, everything that forces me into living "the career."

I've got to tell you man, the worst feeling in the world is when someone is holding you down/back, forcing you to do something you don't want to do, or not allowing you to do something you want to do or something that makes you feel good.

So I decided I needed to do something drastic, to take back my life.

I sent the Madre a letter telling her I don't want her in my life anymore, that I am dead to her. It was a doozy—I'm somewhat apologetic for it, but she's just hurt me too much and too often. I understand she's my mom and all, but <u>flesh and blood are not eternal</u>, so why should I subject myself to so much negativity in this life?

<u>Family</u> are those who support and love one-another, no matter what! I have to say that after sending the letter, a sense of calm settled over me. I feel liberated!

It's amazing what happens when you think of the whole universe as ONE. I mean, I've said it before, several times—the whole transcendental thing, you know, but I've never really thought about what it actually means.

First of all, you realize that death is not for eternity—that we all merge back as One, into the universal spirit.

You also begin to understand that each piece of the whole is as important as the next and that it's up to you to be ONLY who YOU are and not who or what others are or want you to be.

Seriously, imagine a leaf on a tree trying to act like a branch, or a thorn on a rose trying to be the petal. It's never going to happen, and it wouldn't be pretty if it did. So just let it be. It is what it is. Accept it—don't judge—move on, be loving, joyous, and compassionate, and radiate positivity in everything you do.

I love it here, man. This is ME. I _am_ my _Self_ here.

The lotus is blooming! And the universe wants me to dance with it!

Before I left, I heard my mom had been saying stuff like, "I am praying that he finds God."

Well, I tell you what Jack, I've found more than "God" the Father, here. I've found joy, I've found love, I've found myself—my SELF, man. I am MO—Marcus Ortega—part of the One Universe that is all things.

I am in the trees and the mountains, the sunflowers on the beach, and the trickling desert spring. I am in Van Gogh's farmhouses and peasant women and

Michelangelo's David. I am with Whitman and Thoreau, with Redfield in Peru, and I am without fear, without loneliness, for once. I am <u>everywhere</u>!

And Jackson, I am with you <u>ALWAYS</u>.

At the time of this writing, Marc has not taken his own life, and JT says he had never planned to. His letter to his mother was necessary for Marc to release his spirit, to regain control of his own emotions and decisions, and to further become who he truly is. The last JT talked with Marc, although through his father, was to get permission for me to write this book. My hope is that he will emerge again soon and we can finally meet. And let's all hope he is still writing and discovering.